T0209830

Making The Change.

THE DAY IS YOURS. RISE UP & MAKE THE CHANGE.

PENNY MARIPOSA

BALBOA.
PRESS
A DIVISION OF HAY HOUSE

Balboa Press books may be ordered through booksellers or by contacting:

Balboa Press
A Division of Hay House
1663 Liberty Drive
Bloomington, IN 47403
www.balboapress.com
1 (877) 407-4847

Print information available on the last page.

ISBN: 978-1-9822-1718-1 (sc)
ISBN: 978-1-9822-1719-8 (e)

Library of Congress Control Number: 2018914075

Balboa Press rev. date: 12/06/2018

CONTENTS

ACKNOWLEDGMENTS

I want to first take a moment to give recognition to my brother. Who, while completing this book, passed away. My brother had many struggles in his life; he endured a father who did not readily accept him and often undermined him. Sadly, not only did this treatment contribute to a lack of confidence, but in some areas the man he became closely reflected our father. My brother's troubles did not end with his dysfunctional relationship with our father; he experienced many hardships throughout his life and they had a significant hand in preventing him from reaching his full potential. It greatly saddens me that despite being a talented man, his lack of self-worth held him back. I remember as a young girl he used to paint images on my bedroom wall for me, from the yellow submarines by the Beatles, to mushrooms, frogs, and cannabis. He'd inherited our mother's artistic skills and our father's ability to build.

While I attempted to inspire and encourage him to change his life, I recognize that his time in prison served as a major hurdle. Entering the system at a young age for a large portion of his life combined with his alcohol and drug use undoubtedly had a negative impact on his mental development and in some ways, he never truly grew into adulthood. For all my brother's faults, in the end he was simply a good-hearted person who only wanted love and acceptance, a search I too struggled with and it's this similarity that nurtured my connection to him. It's only been a few weeks since his passing and I'm still processing the shock of it. I know I will not only mourn his loss of life, but the life I know he could have lived if he had utilized the untapped well of potential that he possessed and fulfilled his role as an attentive and supportive father and husband.

Nonetheless, while my brother was unable to live up to his potential and pursue the life he wanted, it does not mean that you cannot! But I hope that you might also see, that waiting and prolonging is not an option; if you are reading this book as a means and desire to change your life for the better, do not put it off and do not allow the past to define who you are and who you can become!! While I do believe that it is never too late for us to change no matter our age, I do feel that positive momentums for many of us are needed in the greater scheme of things. Thus, as you read this, become inspired, work towards change, and do one more pivotal thing: No longer put off what you can accomplish today, till tomorrow; instead, make each minute, hour, and day of your life count, because it does!

To the many inspirational motivators, writers, doctors, and help groups (far too many to name but some are mentioned in the book) that work towards paving a new and awakened world, by assisting those in need, inspiring, and encouraging the need for change in each of our personal lives and our society, Thank You. I would not have had the belief that I could make the necessary changes and set forth in life if it were not for your messages and lessons.

To my Daughter,

You have been my rock, my motivation, and my greatest inspiration. I appreciate your honesty, your belief in me, and your unwavering support. You have always been my Angel and I would not be here today had it not been for you being a part of my life. Forever, all my love, Mom.

HELLO AND WELCOME TO
MAKING THE CHANGE!

Change is something I have aspired to for much of my life in one form or another.

Throughout my pursuit, like numerous others, I have read various self-help and inspirational books, which for the most part have proven to be both helpful and encouraging.

However, every now and then, I was left feeling discouraged when I should have been uplifted, primarily due to a crucial aspect missing from their work. I came to realize that the issue rested in my inability to connect with those who had not shared in my experience. The missing puzzle piece turned out to be the history of their hardships; it seemed to me, that a common ground was far more inspirational and motivating. Unfortunately, the spare details that would have offered such confidence, were often conveyed in a positive light. And while, yes, I expect a positive influence when reading this genre, there seems to be a theme of glossing over past traumas and an urge to simply get over the past as opposed to working through them. This approach has ultimately posed a hindrance to my relating to these otherwise uplifting works.

Subsequently, during various college courses, one question repeatedly reared its head. Does a trained professional, even one specialized in the required area, who hasn't shared in similar experiences of any kind ever truly understand their patient/client? Moreover, are they in fact the best suited to aid these individuals in overcoming their problems? This question struck a chord within me, as I couldn't help but correlate this dilemma to the missing aspect that plagued me while reading my self-help books.

For instance, in one class I was asked if the individual who ran AA meetings had more qualifications to aid in recovery than a doctor who had never been an alcoholic. My resounding answer to this was yes; I believe a recovered alcoholic, who can personally relate to the ins and outs of addiction and all the personal and mental trauma that accompanies it, is better equipped to aid a struggling addict, more so than the person who only studied it objectively. So as not to be mistaken, I am not suggesting that trained professionals can't guide and aid us in either recovery or individual growth, in fact my visiting a therapist made a huge leap in my personal development. I merely want to emphasize how we benefit from connecting to those who can relate to our experiences through common ground.

In addition to the lack of commonality with the author, the advice to "just get over it" has been another obstacle in my readings; as I firmly believe in the necessity to sift through and face our past in order to conquer our demons. Several other individuals have further inspired me towards this fact, that I had long believed was essential in truly living life to its fullest. They are mentors promoting people to discover and honestly acknowledge the reason as to why they became stuck in the first place. So that the individual may deeply feel it, relive it, and therefore heal these long-buried wounds, to move forward in life.

Despite this fact, I am in complete agreement with the ideology of *living in the present moment*; I also wholeheartedly believe that until we truly deal with our past issues, moving forward is not an option for the vast majority. Old wounds need to be both acknowledged and then healed, otherwise we risk repeating patterns that we initially sought to change. This, in part, has inspired me to write this book. Therefore, I hope that this writing can assist in first healing deep-rooted wounds and provide you with further insight so that you can *Make the Change* you seek in life.

CHAPTER 1

Lucky Penny

"Lucky Penny" is the nickname given to me by my parents the day I was born and by all outward appearances, I was indeed Lucky. Financially, my parents took good care of me and I am sure I appeared rather spoiled. I can only fathom that my parents enjoyed providing me with all the things they were not privy to when they were children. Both my parents grew up poor; born in the 1930s they grew up during a time of monetary constraints but sought to follow the American tradition of hard work and it paid off. By the time I was about the age of five my parents were doing very well for themselves; my father, with the help of my mother, began his own plumbing company and my mother took on a management position at a local retail store.

Yet something was amiss; although, it would take me a long time to figure out just what it was. Later on, I identified the missing aspects; particularly, not being able to have open, honest, and relevant conversations. Another being each other's supporters as opposed to competitors. Moreover, there was an absence when it came to showing compassion and unconditional love for one another. As well as a lack of being able to express our emotions and in learning how to cope with those emotions.

Eventually, I came to the realization that the significance I had always placed on my name was misdirected towards the word Lucky; instead my new emphasis was on the meaning of the word Penny. As I grew older, I would learn I longed for something different; I had a profound desire for change. However, my primary focus was on changing and fixing others and not so much on myself.

Regardless, I came to be rather independent, divorced at twenty-three years old, raised my beautiful daughter, and did well in my place of work all the while I struggled for years with depression, which began at the age of twelve. During my struggles and in wanting to fix those around me, if anytime I would complain, others would often respond to me with that old familiar affirmation "life isn't fair." That statement never sat well with me. However, they were right; life wasn't fair, and it brought me back to an old poem I had read when I was just a child. Unfortunately, my search over the years to find this extraordinary poem that I remember reading has not come to fruition; nevertheless, I recall the general message, which to this very day has an extremely earnest impact on me. It was in reference to a young child who set out to see the world they had been told of and dreamt of joining. However, while out on their venture the child came to the realization that it was not the world that had been described to them, it was instead a scary, dark place, and thus the child quickly returned home grabbing their coloring book, descending back into their comfort zone. It's hard to convey how and why this poem resonated so deeply within me, nonetheless, to this very moment in time, I can still relate to it.

Additionally, it has furthered my yearning to not abide by some old intrinsic message that had so much power over people in both a destructive and naïve way. For I prefer the wise old sentiment that *life is what we make it*. As a result of this belief, I felt a need to spread my message, thus I am here to tell you, that you have the power to make your life literally whatever you choose it to be! And that it is never too late! We all hold a power to change so many of the injustices we have been told we have little or no control over. Even more so, we have a more significant potential than we have been taught; we all have a purpose here on earth and nothing is ever in vain. It is from our bad experiences that we can actually aid others; instead of hiding these wounds, they can be utilized as an inspirational means to help those who can relate to our bad experiences. Conversely, however, before I could pass this message on to others, I had to find myself first. And so do you, for that matter.

- Take a moment and write down your name.

_____

- Now ask yourself - has it had any notable significance in your life?

_____

_____

_____

3

I asked you to do this because I firmly believe there is something greater than we realize taking place, for I cannot buy into the theory that it is all by chance. Therefore, perhaps our names offer some hidden guidance to our lives. Although, there may be some of you who do not like the name that has been given to you and even others who have actually changed your names because of this unrest. However, such a choice would be indicative of something in and of itself, being that a person would not go to the extent of changing their name if it had not garnished attention to do so.

Take for instance, Nathaniel Hawthorne, it is said that he added the "w" into his last name so that it would not be correlated to his family of origin who were involved in the Salem Witch Trials and the subsequent hanging of many women. Was his decision to separate himself from his family symbolic of how he distinguished himself in society through his writing? In another example, a friend told me a story regarding a woman who once hated her name; in Spanish her name, Nada, meant *nothing* and as a result she was often teased. As the story goes, later in life she met with a man from another country and he relayed to her that her name in his culture meant *spreading the love*. In fact, in many other languages the word Nada means *hope* and in other philosophies it is said to be a vibrational unity with both an inner and outer connection.

While I cannot prove that there is something vaster to this

life we live, just as I cannot disprove much of what science has come to determine as fact, throughout this reading and your life, you might see the constant thread of the opposite sides of life, such as seen on each side of a coin. And the treasure found residing in the middle of it all. What I can say for certain, is that regardless of all the research that has been conducted scientifically, the complexities of our boundless universe tend to lead to more questions than answers. For instance, when we set out with the idea to send man to the moon, we would never have thought for one moment that the rocket and the mission just happened through some sort of evolutionary process with no powerful minds behind it. Powerful minds[1] that we have learned came from women not just men, something not readily relayed to us in our history lessons.

And all the while Science and Religion might be at odds, like that of men and women, rich and poor, white and black, it is in the middle therein lies the truth. Therefore, I know in my heart of hearts and my mind, we too are not here by some form of coincidence - that we, like the planet, may have evolved over time but that it did so for a purpose. Surely there is a reason we are here, an underlying message we have yet to discover. In order for us to awaken it is vital that we heal ourselves, for once those old wounds are healed and we stop the pendulum of repetition, we can continue to further expand, connect, and grow.

---

[1]   http://www.hiddenfigures.com/

Wake Up Call

Following my mother's passing, I began caring for my father. You see, I had made a promise to my mother after receiving bad news from her doctor. During the visit, she was given four months to live; while she was devastated, her primary concern was who would care for our father. That moment is still with me, as I remember her grabbing hold of my hand and asking me "who will take care of Daddy?" I assured her that we would look after him and told her not to worry. While the doctor seemed very eager to provide her with a time frame, he was wrong, and she would stay with us for another year and ten months, passing away on July 11th at 11:11pm.

My father was 83 years old and was in good health for the most part but had recently been having issues with sciatic nerve pain; something I was all too familiar with being that my daughter had been suffering with slipped discs for years. His pain led us to visiting a walk-in clinic, then to the ER where they prescribed a drug for his pain and we then planned a follow up meeting with his VA doctor.

It was August 15th, 2016, a Monday morning; I woke up and got ready to take my father to his VA appointment. When I arrived, his dog was peeking out the window at me and I noticed the door was unlocked, so I let myself in. I knew the moment I opened the door that something was not right; there was a tainted smell. The vase by his lounge chair had fallen, his recliner was still extended with a considerable amount of blood on it. To the left of me, I noticed the kitchen chair was out of place and upon the kitchen counter laid my parent's wedding picture that had been moved from the living room table where it had been placed since my mother's passing, along with other items that were disheveled. I called for him as I walked down the hall, although my gut whispered to me what I was about to discover. As I approached his bedroom I saw his mattress was tilted onto the floor and covered in blood, a few more footsteps and I saw him lying dead on the bathroom floor.

I stood frozen and stared in shock, before calling the police and my daughter. Once they arrived, my daughter and I sat on the front porch as the officials did their job. While waiting, I watched as an extra-large yellow butterfly stayed very close, flying over the plants my parents kept alongside the screened area. As the officer sat down to speak with me, I made the comment that it was my mother, she must have thought I was nuts. However, my mother always had a desire to fly, insisting she would come back to this world as one of the birds or butterflies that she loved so much. Since my mother's passing, those butterflies were present during every visit I had with my father.

Needless to say, I was not prepared to find my father dead; I suppose no one is ever prepared for events like these. What really dug at me was that the day before, I was outside doing yard work alone and I heard a man call my name. I initially associated the voice with that of my brother but the next day when I found my father I knew it had to have been him. I had ignored the phantom voice that called to me, this inner gut feeling. Soon after the police left, my daughter and I headed home; I was ready to drown my sorrows. For my guilt was deep and harsh; I felt frozen. I was angry with myself for ignoring my intuition; I knew better, for far too many times my intuitive messages have proven to have merit.

A few days following his passing, I met up with my brother and his girlfriend who helped me in cleaning the home and arranged a Remembrance Day with his friends. Over the next few months I worked with a realtor and arranged an estate sale, which unfortunately left most of their belongings behind. Family and friends adamantly encouraged me to hold yard sales to move the remainder of their possessions, a prospect I was trying to avoid by hiring an estate planner. Besides the fact that I had never had any success in past attempts of garage sales, being in their home was extremely hard for me, let alone pawning their memories. But despite my misgivings, and once again ignoring my instincts, I set one up for the next weekend.

That morning I awoke early and decided to take dad's dog with me. My father had always worried about who would care for her after he passed, and I had promised to take her in. I walked to his house to meet my family and began preparing for the yard sale. Emotionally, I just couldn't handle it and by just 7am, I began drinking. By noon, I was pretty much oblivious, and I scarcely recall the events that followed. Around 5pm, from what I was told, my family attempted to get me in the car and drive me and the dog home, but I insisted I would walk. Along with a neighbor, she and I walked to the local store that was less than a mile from where we lived. My memory is hazy; however, I do recall seeing no one in the parking lot and thinking "great, I can get in and out quickly." I had never brought an animal in with me before but being that I had been a regular customer for over ten years and seeing no one present, I did not see a problem. However, as soon as I was at the counter a man rushed out asking me to leave. I was already at the counter and I did not understand why they didn't just take my money so that I could go on my way. From the moment he requested I leave, I blacked out and I must have responded rudely, determined not to leave till I got what I had come for, so they called the cops. The combination of my refusal to leave without my purchase and my tripping into the officer due to my flip-flops, lead to my first arrest on 11/11/16. Around 5am the following morning, my daughter came to bail me out and convinced me to quit drinking. Yes, it was time.

For decades, I had attempted, but never succeeded; but then again, maybe I had never really been devoted to the idea of quitting. Although I wanted to quit because of the terrible depression that set in the day after I drank, I cannot say I was ever fully committed. While it was never my intention to cause my daughter emotional turmoil when I drank, I still did so. Sadly, I caused her a lot of stress with my alcohol abuse. Whenever the sudden urge to drink penetrated my system, I rarely contemplated the decision; instead, I allowed my initial impulse to lead the way. While there were moments when I second guessed my instinctual reaction to drink and I talked myself out of it, these instances were few and infrequent. Drinking was something ingrained in my family unit; we always drank, it was a routine, as commonplace as preparing dinner or combing our hair. Regardless of whether I had a choice in the matter, the major problem was that I never took the time to think about not drinking; if my mind and body told me I wanted a drink, I'd leave it at that.

So, in order for me to really commit to the idea of quitting drinking, I knew I would have to come up with a new alternative to my sobriety. I did not feel AA would work for me; I had gone to meetings in the past and I had studied various addiction courses while in college. Nothing had previously worked, or perhaps I just never wanted it to. Nevertheless, I decided to come up with my own method. After taking a penetrative look into my past behavior, we identified that a primary obstacle for me in choosing sobriety was giving it conscious thought. Every day my daughter and I would discuss why I was sober, the positives and the negatives. In the past, I had written down the pros and cons of drinking; the positives amounted to one – it made me feel good by releasing my anxiety and tension, and the negatives were an endless myriad of reasons not to. Obviously, this approach still inspired little devotion in me, I would need something more engaging. So, we took time every day, morning and night to discuss my drinking and it ended up being a beneficial idea. Of course, I cannot say for certain what worked, was it just that I was committed this time, or was it the method we used? Maybe both. Or maybe the idea of 5 years in prison for a felony on an officer and leaving my daughter all alone was just a major wake up call.

Regardless, I set out to quit; together we had our daily conversations and I continued to see my therapist along with taking Zoloft for my depression. That Christmas my daughter bought me chalk boards to go around the home, on which she wrote my favorite motivational quotes, along with a *YOU are a BADASS* calendar and inspirational posters. All the while paying specific attention to my triggers, which for me could be any minor little issue that arose. Boy, could I make a mountain out of a molehill. I mean one little thing could make my anxiety skyrocket, instantly provoking my desire to down my favorite cold beverage.

I made it through the fall without a glitch; school began again in January, it would be my final semester. By the end of March, I got my parents' home sold and by May completed writing my first book. We continued to have our conversations twice a day and each time the conversation grew more thorough, revealing a deeper understanding about my relationship with alcohol. April 5th, I had an appointment to see my psychiatrist, then on to pay my probation bill. My daughter waited for me in the car for about 45 minutes when I came rushing out ready to leave; I was in a wretched mood. We stopped by a local store to pay the probation but there was an issue with the payment machine. The employee's attempt to fix the issue took another 30 minutes before informing us it couldn't be resolved, so we headed onwards to our next chore. On our way I made the comment, "we should just go home it's not a good day." Alas, I did not follow my gut nor was I present in the moment.

After a pile of small annoyances at our next stop, I had finally paid my probation in full, handed the cashier the ticket and watched as the clerk crumpled up the receipt to throw away. My blood boiled. I needed that receipt! At the time I had his pen in my hand and the cashier told me to give it back; obstinately I demanded my receipt and threw in the F-word. A customer walking by called out to me to watch my language, not a comment I wanted to hear in my terrible mood. I replied to her that it was my constitutional right under the 1st amendment, while the cashier continued to demand the pen I held in my hand. Now I'll admit I've been known to be a pen thief when I come across one I love, but in this instance, that wasn't the case. I was getting irritated that he was so concerned about his cheap pen rather than settling the transaction by providing my receipt for over a thousand dollars that I was required to deliver to my probation officer. This interaction was the last I could stand after a day of nonstop aggravations. By the evening my anxiety was running high and that night I didn't sleep. By Friday that week, my anxiety was still out of control and once my daughter left for work I made the decision to drink.

I said to myself, "what would a few beers hurt?" I needed to relieve this tension. Shortly after she left, I called a taxi and purchased my favorite alcohol. I can still envision the very first sip, and the relief I felt instantly, but within minutes I became lost to the world. I apparently took another taxi ride to purchase another four pack, however I had no memory of what occurred after that first sip. It's not normal for me to blackout so incredibly quickly and I would assume the same for most people. Knowing that I could blackout so rapidly was not only frightening but ironically, a sobering thought. The last thing I needed was to once again not be in control and land myself in trouble while on probation for a felony. Surely, no one would believe I could have blacked out so soon, because they didn't even believe it during my arrest.

Despite my slip, I finally reached my year minus a day of being sober. Instead of beginning again after my relapse, I decided to use 'minus a day' as opposed to starting from scratch. It made me feel more positive and didn't induce that black hole that consumes you when an addict once again experiences failure. Throughout this time, I have learned to identify and control my triggers, and my desire to drink was not as intense as it once was. In due course, day-by-day, the desire to drink grew less and less relevant, with minor passing thoughts, whereas my ultimate focus was to get busy.

It was time for me to find my destiny and live up to my potential. My mother's words still in my head, telling me I would "go on to do something great one day." Being the only family member in the end to care for my parents once they passed, it felt like it was my time, my time to leave the past behind me and to truly focus on my life's purpose and future. It was as if their deaths had to happen in order for me to move on in life. I owed it to my daughter as well, for far too long she bore the brunt of the chaos and turmoil of my family. I always put them before her, forced her to deal with them even though she was much happier and content with it being just the two of us. What can I say, I had a deep sense of commitment when it came to family; for my entire life they were my worldview, there existed nothing outside of them. But now, it was my time, and it was time to be present in the moment and finally pursue my goals!

Take a moment to reflect on your life.

- What changes are you trying to make in your life?

_____

_____

_____

_____

_____

- Have you experienced any "wake up call" moments?

_____

_____

_____

_____

_____

- If so, did they result in any change on your part or in your life?

_____

_____

_____

_____

_____

- If not, why do you think nothing changed?

_____

_____

_____

_____

_____

It's not a new concept to write these things down and you might find it an unnecessary task but taking the time to ask ourselves these questions often prompts us to either make discoveries about ourselves or evaluate things we never thought to give much mind to.

Intuitive Messages

What does intuition mean? It is defined as a perception that has substantial meaning. Animals live by their intuitive messages; when watching a deer, one might notice them suddenly stop chewing, raise their head, and gaze out at their surroundings, as they take a moment to be conscious of what it is they are feeling. An apparent warning bell goes off, alerting them to pay attention. They live in the state of the moment and are genuinely dependent on these natural instincts in order to survive.

Our five senses as humans are described as sight, taste, touch, smell, and sound. But the sixth sense is not often discussed. And yet, this inner knowing that often comes out of nowhere happens to be a common occurrence that we all experience throughout our lifetime. Our intuition can be rather spooky, particularly once proven that the message had actual merit. For the most part we downplay these occurrences and dismiss them as pure happenstance. However, if we gave them the proper credence, we may find it to be a helping hand. Why else would we have this ability?

Intuition often seems to defy our perception of reality, giving us an awareness that we can't reasonably explain. How far does it extend beyond us? Could it be possible that nature, from our smallest wildlife to the far reaches of the solar system, is not only in tune with these messages but lives accordingly? While this is out of my expertise, many studies from people like Dean Radin, Rupert Sheldrake, Graham Hancock, Nassim Haramein, and Leonard Susskind (among many others who have dedicated their lives to studying these fascinating topics) insinuate that there is much more behind the scenes than we realize.

- What are your views on intuition? Do you believe in it?

_____

_____

_____

_____

_____

My Experience With Intuitive Messages

Over the years I have had multiple messages come my way. Like most people, I at first discounted them, or may not have given them much credibility. Looking back now, however, the deep-rooted feelings or messages that reared their head had a weight that I know to be undeniable.

A few years prior to my sister's death, she and I were speaking on the phone; she was going through a hard time separating from her longtime companion and father of her children. While on the phone I felt a presence, it came down my hall into my kitchen where I was sitting, a pot resting on the dish rack fell to the floor, my dog began barking, and my daughter's rocking chair began swaying. I instinctually associated the presence with my Aunt Marie, whom I had never met personally as she died of cancer while my mother was pregnant with me. I felt the message I was receiving was a warning that something bad was on the way. Two years later my sister would be diagnosed with cancer and she'd appeared woeful to the fact that our mother gave her the middle name Marie.

Prior to my mother's illness, I had a constant message flowing through me. I had broken ties with my family for a time; throughout the summer of 2013, I was awoken by a message that insisted that I reconnect with my family – for time is running out. It still gives me chills just recalling it as I write this. In August, I had my mother over for coffee so that we could put aside our differences and move forward. That Fall my mother found out she had a tumor located behind her heart and in front of her lungs that could not be surgically removed. Fortunately, we reconnected and resolved some of our issues before it was too late; she eventually passed away on July 11th, 2015. I chose not to attend the funeral as to avoid family drama and mourn alone; instead my daughter and I stayed the night at a hotel. I was drinking that night, thinking of my mom, down by the pool. It was after swimming hours when I decided to take a dip. The staff attempted to get me out of the pool, but I just kept swimming. Not much later, the police arrived - four of them to be exact. While they escorted me to my room, I tripped in the process and accidently bumped into a male officer. I'm not normally agile in the first place, so being inebriated in flip-flops was bound to be a bad combination. I can only assume he thought it was intentional as his response was to threaten that I could be charged with a felony on a police officer. Luckily, the female officer de-escalated the situation, recognizing it for the accident it was. Realizing how easily my actions while drinking could endanger my life with the law, I promised my daughter I would quit drinking. It was another in a long line of failed promises, as I had been drinking since the age of 12 years old and was then 44.

A year and four months later, I had ironically encountered an incredibly similar event that had occurred following my father's passing, only this time I wouldn't be escaping scot-free. It was November 11, 2016 that I was arrested. I couldn't help but find the date significant, as it matched the exact moment of my mother's passing, 11:11pm. Could these numbers have any value to them? Who would have thought a year later, following the passing of another parent, I would actually get arrested for nearly the same incident that occurred a year before? Was it a message for me to quit drinking?

I might never know for certain, but I did know that it was indeed time to make some changes and it began with removing alcohol from my life. Not to mention, I could not again ignore my intuition or the repetitive coincidences that occurred, as they were anything but. The experience cemented my belief that the universe sends us messages, we must only be open to the possibility and heed the warning. And my point of sharing my story with others is in hopes that you too will become in tune with your inner source and pay attention to them as they come to you. This makes the concept of being in the moment even more significant, as not all these messages may be so persistent.

- Have you had any experience with intuitive messages?

_____

_____

_____

_____

_____

•   Did you consider these messages meaningful or
    worthy of attention?

_____

_____

_____

_____

_____

•   Are you attempting to live in the moment so that
    you can acknowledge these messages when they come
    to you?

_____

_____

_____

_____

_____

Life's Purpose

Unfortunately, I do not have the pleasure at this very moment to know about you, the reader; but if you are reading this, then perhaps you and I share something in common. For me, it took years to discover my life's purpose. While it may have been right in front of me the entire time, I just could not seem to figure it out. What I did possess was the gift of gab, boy could I talk up a storm. Sadly, I was also very good at wasting time or had the lack of energy to utilize it wisely.

For much of my adult life, I did not acquire that get-up-and-go attitude that my other family members had been blessed with. I was part of the Generation Xers and as we have noticed, new generations have gained quite the distinction in the areas of traditional values and social norms. Regardless, while I may have held an appreciation for hard work and still do today, I suffered from pure exhaustion. Once I came home from work I could barely keep up with all the other 'to dos' on my list, such as being a mother and homecare provider. But amidst the hurdles of keeping pace with the demands of single motherhood, in the back of my mind, I had the suppressed desire to find the path back to the child I once was and all the ambition and joy that accompanied it.

Repeatedly I'd ask myself, "what happened to that girl?" The one that as soon as her eyes would open come morning, she would spring from the bed eager to start the day. Then come the evening, my parents had a hard time reining me in for the night to prepare for bed. Undoubtedly, the majority of us can recall such times, as that boundless energy is synonymous with childhood.

But beyond that, I longed for that ambition and the excitement of life that somewhere along the way had been lost.

• Do you recall what your aspirations were when you were young?

_____

_____

_____

_____

_____

Alas, one day something changes; reality sets in and there are all these things we must do in order to survive, caught up in the day-to-day challenges of getting by, making ends meet, and going along with the norm. During my studies in sociology, I discovered I had conflicting viewpoints in regards to our social structure. While it made sense to have developed this social organization, such as certain standards to follow, live by and such, it also bothered me in the control it had, its undermining quality, and the narrow-minded tunnel vision it ensured. We grow comfortable and even complacent with the social norms, caught up in stuff that actually has little relevance to our life. Adventuring into the unknown is not as spry as it once was, when we were in our youth. Sadly, due to the means of survival, many of us cannot follow our life's purpose. We end up stuck in jobs that we hate and a path that was not meant for us. Struggling day-by-day just to make it by. Trying to keep up with the latest advances and fitting into a very monetary orientated world.

At some point during this bombardment, I lost my desire to pursue life, but I never gave up my longing to change. I felt like a disappointment most of the time, because while my desire to change was strong, I just seemed to lack the ability and energy to do so. Partly, I would say it was due to my emotional roller coaster, driven by my depression and alcoholism, which always ended at the same destination - failure. I failed time and time again, repeating the same old pattern while never learning the lesson that was necessary for me to *make the change* I needed in order to flourish.

- Consider your own life for a moment. Can you identify any parallels between my struggles and yours?

_____

_____

_____

_____

_____

- Take a moment and contemplate what in your life is holding you back from meeting your potential. It could be anything from your energy or lack thereof, family, job, or self-belief. Take time to evaluate these all-encompassing reasons.

_____

_____

_____

_____

_____

Even with my setbacks, I still held steadfast in the idea of transforming our lives. Unfortunately, for quite some time my focus was misdirected upon others rather than myself. I wanted those I loved to change; I wanted to fix them, to fix what was wrong with the situation we found ourselves in. It propelled me into relentless discussions concerning growth with my loved ones that routinely ended in disappointment on my behalf, often hearing the argument that there comes a time when one is too old to change. I struggled with accepting this concept as it was in direct opposition to what I hoped for myself. While I am by no means a perfectionist in regard to transformation, there were several areas in my life that I wanted to improve.

It is never too late to change your life, just look at the founder of the publishing company through which provided you this book. Louise Hay wrote her first book *Heal Your Body* at age 50. Tim Gunn did not become a big-time sensation until the age of 51 when he began working on Project Runway. While I only take time to name two, there are a myriad of people who find their way and soul's purpose later on in life. Many of whom we may not have heard of... yet, or many we may never have the fortune of knowing. Nonetheless, there is nothing wrong with getting started later in life and yet there are many things that can hold us back from our life's pursuit or in learning what our true destiny is. If you are reading this now and longing to find your destination...consider this your time! Just know that it is truly never too late to start.

As I mentioned, it's both reassuring and inspiring to look towards others who have faced obstacles similar to our own or have accomplished shared dreams despite adversity. Do some research and make a list of these people.

- In what ways, specifically, is their story inspiring?

_____

_____

_____

_____

_____

- What are the similarities you share?

_____

_____

Acknowledging the triumphs despite hardships made by others can help strengthen our own resolve. After a continuous internal struggle and much studying, I came to realize that our greatest obstacle is indeed without a doubt - Our State of Mind. If you believe you can't do it, then you can bet on your life ~ you won't. Nobody has ever become successful when immersed in doubt; great performers did not get up on stage thinking "OMG I suck!!" Now, this is not to say they don't have some uncertainty, we all do, but it is the percentage of that self-doubt vs. the percentage of self-confidence that matters. This mental battle is perfectly represented by the classic metaphor of an angel and devil on opposing shoulders, influencing our lives. It's imperative to one's success that you direct your attention towards the angel so that you may tip the balance in your favor, enhancing your self-belief into becoming an unmistakable WOW moment of your life! An important prelude to obtaining that self-confidence is discovering your niche, which can be a struggle in and of itself for some but take the time to write down your strengths.

Come back to this list and consider your ideas. It may take time to truly find that path; I know it did for me. While I always knew that I wanted to help others, I was unsure of how to go about it. I worked for years at a courthouse, then a police department before leaving to pursue my real ambitions, but not yet truly sure of what that precisely was. I began with a company that helped children with disorders, while also working with people who hoarded as a life coach, but again I was trying to change others, not myself. I decided to go back to school, an experience I greatly enjoyed as it gave me the opportunity to delve into subjects such as religion, our history, women's movements, and philosophy, which I hadn't ever studied in-depth before. My classes also reinforced my stance against the laws and social rules that we are born into as a society. I'm not the type to do things conventionally and I believe conforming to social norms can be a damper to finding real happiness. So, I encourage you to find avenues that speak to you and conform to your path, rather than the other way around.

Making our dreams into reality is not always an easy task and more often than not seems impossible. That doubt can be debilitating, which is why I encourage the mindset of focusing solely on the essence of what you want to achieve. At times it's easy to get distracted by everyday life and the superficial things that mean absolutely nothing in the grand scheme. Really make the commitment to filter out the petty interferences that warp our priorities and waste our precious time. And while time is essential to life, you must know that it is never too late to find your destiny and pursue it. For all the while time is vital to us, it is also just an illusion. Many studies believe that there is no such thing as time, that the past, present, and future are all connected and happening at this very moment, even though we are not able to see it this way.

Point being, and to rehash, it is never too late to change; change is why we are here, it is part of our creation, it is our purpose, and the main reason for existing. Many of us struggle with finding our path in life, not the one that would be most useful but the one that brings us fulfillment. Miraculously, one day I came across this quote from Martin Luther a professor of theology and a German monk from Germany born in 1483. He stated, *"If you want to change the world, pick up your pen and write."* That quote resonated with me. I mean, I had the gift to gab after all, so why not put my words in writing? And so, I did.

- Do you know what your sole purpose is here today? Take a moment to write down what you think it is, and what you want it to be.

_____

_____

_____

_____

_____

- Whatever it is, pay attention the next few days ahead; keep your desire close to your thoughts and heart and take notice of any messages that may come your way. Write them down, review them, take time to feel what they mean to you and explore further in depth what path you were meant to pursue!

_____

_____

_____

_____

_____

CHAPTER 2

Upbringing

For decades, there has been a great debate over what matters more, nature or nurture. It is yet another common argument we have in our world that pits one ideal against another, without taking under consideration that both are not only plausible but also paramount to our lives. Evidence has proven that it is not one or the other, but rather that both play an essential part of our existence. This should be expected for those of us who believe that the balance of life is a significant factor in how we evolve. Even though our genetics can influence our health and behavior, more research has proven that other factors can overcome and alter what many have come to believe as just hereditary.[2]

From the beginning of our existence, the way in which we are treated, mentored, and the environment that surrounds us has an extreme impression on our development physically, mentally, and spiritually. Yet, the idea that parenting needs to be taught is often swept aside, or we have expectations

---

[2]   To learn more, I highly recommend *Biology of Belief*, Bruce H. Lipton, Ph.D. presents great information regarding placebo effects, and the correlation of genetics with our subconscious mind.

that our parents will train us properly as their parents trained them and so on. Bringing our children into the world has been chalked down to traditions, undermined in its importance, and even dismissed as a natural endeavor, not in need of a deeper understanding or worthy of training. Even though numerous people have changed their opinion on how to nurture our youth, it is still commonplace *to spare the rod and spoil the child*, known to many as the traditional quote passed down from Proverbs. Usually, when our children have done something wrong, the result is a spanking. A physical method used in order to teach a mental lesson. Although I am not here to teach lessons on proper parenting, I do want to make note of just how incredibly powerful this job is and the substantial effect it plays both on our own destiny and others.

Whatever occurs during our childhood will influence us ~ conditioning both our physical and mental state of being. Various things we might be taught in order to survive, such as how we respond to situations that arise, what is considered to be right or wrong, how we communicate, and how we care for others and ourselves, is fundamental in teaching us our coping skills. Our upbringing has the ability to create abuse, suffering, and pain, but it also has the power to open the doors for a remarkable destiny that we might not even be able to conceive in its entirety.

Sometimes the conditions our upbringing creates can be so subtle that we may not recognize them until much later in life, if ever. I, for example, have always struggled with self-discipline. A fact that I found puzzling as my parents had such a strong work ethic. It eventually dawned on me that my occasional struggle with motivation likely stemmed from having little responsibility as a child. This shows how a seemingly insignificant misstep in parenting can have such a resounding influence later in life. While interest and consideration for child development is markedly more widespread today, even self-aware families can cause undesirable behaviors down the line. I say this only because if there is something in your life you are attempting to change and it's a battle to do so, you may benefit from trying to identify the source of your issue. Those who have had a pleasant childhood may be less likely to consider it when facing a persisting dilemma later in life. Unfortunately, there are many who have not been raised with their wellbeing in mind and their obstacles often reflect that fact.

While we have no control over our birth and to whom we are born, we do have the power to heal old wounds and learn from our experiences. Therefore, at this point in time we should be focused on ourselves and finding a way to mend past trauma so that we can grow from any injustices we may have suffered. There is no doubt that many who have endured similar or worse mistreatment have paved a great life for themselves and become sources of inspiration. Ones we turn to for healing, enlightenment, and encouragement so that we too might live a better life. Unfortunately, however, not everyone can or knows how to overcome adversity. Many become stuck, end up addicted, in trouble, or controlled by emotions. Alas, any trauma we may have encountered is often times dismissed, undermined, or we are told *to get over it*. This common response to our pain is yet another example of an old lesson passed down from generation to generation.

In retrospect, it is easy to see why this has become a common occurrence; for looking at our history, the suffrage and pain endured is unimaginable and for the most part we do not see this happenstance reoccurring today. Our current generations are looked at as the lucky ones, with little understanding to the hardships that were not only endured but hidden away for means to survive and in some cases, flourish. All in the effort to provide the life we are fortunate enough to be living today. Now of course, this is not true for all families; sadly, there are still a lot of bad things happening in many of our lower, impoverished communities, not to mention other countries that still lay dormant in the face of progress, weighed down by controversy, control, and unrest.

Nevertheless, our ancestors no doubt bore a much harder way of life than most of us do today. And while I admire the tenacity of older generations which allowed them to power through their trials, I also recognize that they were stilted in overcoming their demons in a healthy way. It was not that long ago that any and all family issues were expected to be locked away behind closed doors, preventing any opportunity to seek outside help. Even with the leaps and bounds made in transparency, especially where social media is concerned, it's still a stigma that persists today. The beliefs surrounding our sequestered lives that existed decades ago has lived on; we see it in the attitude of those that dismiss people's past ordeals and consider the need to work through it a weakness.

It has become known as re-victimization, centered around the old school of thought that people should just get over it. However, we shouldn't undermine someone by not empathizing with them and their life experience and at the same time we want them to not stay stuck in it. But it is essential that if they are to heal, then they and their story should be recognized. Keeping someone from sharing their experience because they want them to 'build a bridge and get over it,' does not erase the truth but rather leads to the replication of unhealthy and damaging cycles. Our children are a product of the environment we provide for them and if we remain quiet about abuse, they too will learn to stay quiet.

While I am an advocate for facing our past injuries, don't mistake it for the approval of dwelling. We do not want these traumas to take hold of us and have control to the point where we repeat patterns or live in a constant state of 'woe is me.' Once more, we can see not only the need for balance in one's life but the crucial value it holds. Confronting our past traumas and inner demons is a means in which we can genuinely grow as an individual; we cannot honestly evolve and adapt if we continue to deny the existence of meaningful moments in our life, regardless of how painful they may be.

Opening up to others about our doubts and struggles is a valuable tool in recovery but finding someone to confide in is not always a simple matter. Family, those who we often think would be the natural selection, are not always the healthiest option; a mistake I personally made. On my path to personal growth, which involved thorough analyzing of myself, upbringing, and familial relationships, I reached out to my family for support. What I got in response was a barrage of criticism. I was repeatedly told, "there's something wrong with you" and "you're the problem in this family and everyone knows it." At a time when I was emotionally fragile and in turmoil over my past, I internalized this feedback and believed they were right, it was me. To an extent they were correct, at least in the sense that I was different than them. I was of a wholly separate mindset. I had reached a point in my life where I needed to self-reflect and face hard truths and my family was not equipped to deal with my push for honesty. Looking back now it seems obvious that I shouldn't have looked to the source of many of my issues - my dysfunctional family - for support, especially since they were still embroiled in it themselves.

However, I could not do this on my own, so I found a therapist to help me; I purposely looked for a woman of my age. Of course, who you find to assist you is your decision but know that you should find someone that you will feel comfortable with, someone that you will be able to relate to, and a person that you can trust to express your most profound truth and deepest secrets.

- How would you characterize your childhood?

_____

_____

_____

_____

_____

• What was your family structure like?

_____

_____

_____

_____

_____

• Did you take on any roles that helped shape who you are? I.e. a fixer, listener, scapegoat, hero, etc.

_____

_____

_____

_____

_____

• Did you grow out of the role or are still entrenched in it?

_____

_____

_____

_____

_____

- If so, how does it affect your life today?

_____

_____

_____

_____

_____

Addictions

Even for a normal, well-adjusted individual, changing one's life can be a challenge. Now add an addiction to the mix and it can seem daunting at best. While we may be unaware of our own, a significant portion of society suffers from some form of addiction. You may have heard it before, but without a doubt, addictions are all-encompassing, ranging from the seemingly innocuous to soul-crushing chasms. Regardless of the degree of dependency, there is always an incentive behind it and in the cases of life-consuming addictions, there is no greater catalyst than our past. Addictions are often something that we pursue, as a consequence of events that occurred during our history; perhaps you were denied something, neglected, bullied, or a victim of abuse. The residual turmoil of emotions that we experience as a result, compels us to seek a solution to that stress, pain, or emptiness through artificial means. Other times substance abuse is brought on by an accident, in which we are prescribed a prescription drug in order to help relieve the pain.

As I mentioned, addictions are panoptic in nature and can occupy both ends of the good/bad spectrum. When the majority of us hear the word addiction, we automatically picture someone strung out from drugs or alcohol; for a great deal of functioning society this is not the case, thus making it difficult to identify an issue. We've all heard of people addicted to exercise or of workaholics and usually we make light of these labels because they seem harmless enough in the grand scheme of things.

On the other hand, a lack of balance can easily affect the quality of one's life and should not be overlooked; even healthy habits can grow into obsessive behavior given the right conditions. Work, for example, can come between loved ones causing strain on relationships as well as preventing a person from joining in on life's other experiences. Consequently, those we love may feel diminished due to our careers or other dominating desires that take precedence over all else. Unlike damaging substances such as street drugs where there is a ready awareness of the potential for addiction, our everyday habits can slowly take over our lives without any warning. These everyday routines can quickly mature into dependencies for a variety of reasons as they develop in such a way that we may not know it is a problem until someone points it out to us.

In his book, *The Power of Now,* Eckhart Tolle describes how our thoughts can become an addiction. This is a concept I can wholeheartedly relate to; for our brain resembles a machine but with no off switch, an annoyance I am sure I'm not alone in experiencing. For we tend to overthink and become encumbered by the racing of our thoughts. We become entangled in them, allowing them to rule us. Our minds are powerful tools, even more so than machines in some respects. However, while we have control over our technology, it can often seem as if that control does not extend towards our own minds. It's a daunting thought but not a surprising one for anyone who has struggled with either restraint or discipline. When we avoid taking command of ourselves, we are not living in a state of awareness; it is essential that we make our conscious-self take the reins.

Today, many have fallen prey to the habit of binging, whether it's through social media, texting, gaming, or TV; it has become a primary obstacle, especially for today's youth. Technology has brought the ability to connect to millions around the world in moments and yet ironically, if we allow it to, it can also impede our personal relationships outside of the internet. While I am personally not one deeply involved in social media, I can understand how it can be so addictive. There are times when I am online reading tweets and just become engulfed in the event that is taking place. However, while we may want to stay connected to what is going on in the world, we do not want to become consumed by it.

In a society where consumerism runs rampant, it's not surprising that materialism is also a burgeoning source of addiction as well. When you couple this fact with the pressure to meet certain standards, especially from social media that is always at our fingertips, what other outcome could be expected? Everyone is familiar with the term 'shopaholic,' someone who consumes more and more to seek that comfort or fill that void that any other addict experiences. However, this concept has evolved to not just need more *things* but a *lifestyle* or rather at least the appearance of one. Corny though it may sound, there is something to be said of the simple things in life and the importance to our health in not allowing a disconnect to form between the material and what is *real*.

It takes a great deal of self-discipline and self-determination to live a well-balanced life, even more so when it was not instrumental in our upbringing. I want to emphasize the importance of moderation; a concept which seems ridiculously simple yet is a struggle I have shared in for much of my life. I, like many people in our world, struggle with what others might consider to be ordinary daily routine, but to me seemed more like a balancing act that was constantly on the verge of tipping. I also had the bad habit of throwing all of myself into a task, even to the point of overexertion while at other times I could barely summon the interest. Nevertheless, I have longed to live a modest lifestyle. Knowing without a doubt that balance was not only essential but genuinely the way life was meant to be lived.

Point being, is that anything can grow to be an addiction when we do not consume it in a healthy, modest way. When we succumb to it, nothing will ever be enough; it only feeds on itself and grows, exacerbating the issue. Overconsumption becomes our safety net, our routine, and our comfort zone. Unfortunately, that comfort it offers is nothing more than an illusion, which lasts as long as the high. For this reason, we cannot and will not ever find real freedom, comfort, or relief until we come to this realization.

My addictions over the years ranged from binge drinking, eating, to TV. In so far as my binging, I never knew how to stop after one drink or even two for that matter; it was always the entire pack, maybe more, and I always drank until I passed out. Despite my addiction, internally, I held a sincere desire to change. My constant drinking that lasted 34 years weighed me down considerably. I always awoke the next day in a devastating depression, which would often not subside for weeks at a time. Afterwards, once my motivation set in, the energetic rush would lead to anxiousness and just like that I was drinking again to relieve the tension.

It was an endless spiral, leaving me so discouraged in any belief that I could ever change my life. Consequently, I was left in a mindset that a person like me, who failed so many times as I had, should just give up already, just accept things as they were and deal with it. However, as I write this today, I am sober one year, and 10 months - minus a day. In April of 2017, I had a relapse; while most programs have their members start from scratch in counting their sobriety, I decided to mentally minus a day instead. Anyone who has encountered the cycle of failure, understands how debilitating and discouraging it is to fail once again. I knew that if I wanted to succeed in my sobriety I needed to build up my confidence by giving myself props for what I had achieved instead of laying so much emphasis on my relapse.

I feel encouraged and proud when I say I have been sober for almost 2 years minus a day, as opposed to starting over and essentially throwing away all the progress and the benefits along with it. This may sound trivial, but it truly made all the difference in my attitude in maintaining my drive for a sober life, a stark difference to the complete lack of determination I'd feel during the depression that always followed my falls. It came to be more than just rephrasing my sobriety status; rather, I was willing to forgive myself instead of punishing myself. Herein lies a significant part to my writing; while it's common and expected that we look towards either the established methods of recovery or the ideology of others with authority, remember that there is no "one size fits all" solution. Not everything works for everyone, so I implore you to experiment and find what works best for you; this may mean taking parts from different philosophies and piecing them together or developing a method unique to you and your situation.

Either way, many of us struggle with these addictions when in turn life was meant to be lived by modest means. Whatever the addiction, it is often used as a coping mechanism to deal with an underlying yet no less prevalent factor, that most likely for too long has gone unacknowledged, and if one is to change their lives, it is pertinent to get a grasp on it. This is not always an easy feat, but it can be more comfortable than we make it if we are genuinely committed. When you feel the urge to resort to your addiction, try to recognize the reason for your impulse; be sure to write it down so to remember it. Take a few deep breaths to attempt to relax your state of mind and if possible seek an alternate method to divert your current set of emotions. A method I often turn to is cleaning, as a means of releasing my energy and emptying my mind. I did this especially as a means to escape my depression, turning the music on and cleaning was a way to distract me from my emotional state at the moment.

As previously mentioned, it is vital that we acknowledge that not one thing will cure us all; there are many avenues we can utilize to change our direction. Sadly, a majority of courts today, demand that people with addictions attend AA programs. In my studies on addictions, we were presented with various ways people might utilize alternative techniques to improve, for there is not one full proof method; the good news is there really are more options than told to us. Therefore, I cannot stress enough that you take the time to learn the right fix for you. But even more so, know that addictions are not cured overnight. Most people do and will have relapses, so be prepared for them; make certain if by chance you have one, to do it in the safest manner possible. For years we have looked towards our politicians, judges, and policies for quick fixes, but there is no such thing, and because of this need that would never transpire we have instead dropped further into the rabbit hole.

Additionally, if you are experiencing depression, anxiety, fear, or any type of disorder and you use alcohol or drugs as a means of relief, don't expect that you'll be able to solve one without broaching the other. These duos become so closely entwined, that at times it's hard to know where one stops and another begins. The drugs and alcohol we utilize for our pain and our need to escape is nothing more than a vicious cycle that we will not cure until we are honest with ourselves and gain the ability to seize the day and moment at hand. While recovery is never an easy process and more than likely one will fail once, twice, or many times prior to actually achieving victory, know this, it comes down to one thing and one thing only, your state of mind. According to research for the Intervention Program the statistical rate of recovery is 55%. Unfortunately, the government does not implement studies on recovery programs that are usually mandated by the courts, but nonetheless, I am here to tell you that recovery isn't a distant dream. Now why would you believe me? I have no prior teaching in recovery but what I do have is sobriety; I grew up drinking and doing drugs from the age of twelve and it continued until late in life. I have been addicted to many things during my lifetime, but I reined it all in and I know that You Can Too! It all comes down to one very simple decision, your choice to stop, and from there the decision to be conscious of your mind, in control of it at all times.

There is no doubt that when pursuing recovery, relapsing is a common occurrence; we might fail three, four, or even ten times before we actually succeed. This truth that recovery can take longer than we want, or others expect of us can be very discouraging. Today, we hear people talking about giving those who made a mistake a second chance in life, but those of us who are addicted may need more than just second chances. Relapsing is natural, so do not lose your hope; recovery is attainable, and it really amounts to your control over your state of mind. And if I can do it, You Can Do It! You just need to make the decision to do so; it isn't always easy but is nevertheless possible.

- For those not experiencing addiction, are there any struggles with imbalance in your life? What are they?

_____

_____

_____

_____

_____

- Have you become addicted to anything over the years?

_____

_____

_____

_____

_____

- If yes, what are they and how long have you been addicted?

_____

_____

_____

_____

_____

- What are the repercussions? On you (mentally, physically, mentally) and your relationships.

_____

_____

_____

_____

_____

- Have you taken any steps to get help and if so what were they?

_____

_____

_____

_____

_____

- Can you identify the urge that drives you to your addiction?

_____

_____

_____

_____

_____

- If you haven't achieved recovery, can you identify any specific reasons why?

_____

_____

_____

_____

_____

- What steps can you take to combat them?

_____

_____

_____

_____

_____

Emotions

While it is our emotions that undeniably make life worth living, there are also many times we curse their overwhelming nature. It is expected that as an adult we have control over our emotions and therefore the actions they dictate. However, there are more individuals ill-equipped in their coping manners than we may expect. Also, if you are struggling with stress, anxiety, depression, fear, anger, or other incapacitating emotions, there is no need to feel less than; for you are not alone. For those of us who were raised without the instruction of coping skills, wayward emotions have a greater tendency to influence our actions. And we are often susceptible to turning towards the bottle or other addictive variants to 'cope' with our feelings in lieu of handling them in a healthy manner. Regrettably, this inclination is, to say the least, counterproductive and furthers the cycle of destructive emotions while also slowly destroys any healthy thought processes we do possess.

Not everyone appreciates the power of thought and even fewer acknowledge the damage we can do to ourselves with negativity. For those who are in an unhealthy frame of mind, simply overthinking a situation can lead to excessive worry and then to the paralyzing feeling of being overwhelmed, further hindering the path to progress. I merely want to point out the necessity of gaining control over our emotions, so that they don't control us. Some mistakenly believe that the answer to this is to repress our feelings and experiences. But not only is this an unhealthy solution, it doesn't work. If the emotion is powerful enough, one will unwittingly exhibit signs that reflect what they are suppressing, whether if it's in how they treat others or themselves, mentally or physically. Unfortunately, it's not uncommon for this misconception to be taught during childhood.

For instance, some of us might have been taught not to cry or show any emotion under the guise of it being a weakness. In contrast, others were given no direction as to how to control their emotions; so much so, that our feelings end up ruling us and every facet of our lives. The latter had a heavy hand in how I was raised, for we expressed our emotions over all else, even when it interfered with our relationships, jobs, and the ability to cope with life's infinite trivial events that go awry. The prospect of reteaching ourselves fundamental skills is an intimidating one, but despite how you may have been raised and the journey that has led you to your current state, know, it is never too late to change. Don't give credence to those idioms "a leopard doesn't change its spots" or "you can't teach an old dog new tricks." Such phrases are used by the exact mindset that is holding you back.

Overall, our emotions come about us rather subconsciously. These sensations can come on fast with little to no warning, like an instant jolt of lightning penetrating throughout our being. At times our feelings can be painful, but they can also be amazing, either way - to feel - is to experience life in depth!

Our emotions should not be buried even when they are hurtful and yet, they were not meant to control us, weigh us down, or govern our lives. We must not ignore our emotions for fear of the pain and discomfort, for doing so actually empowers them. Therefore, it is both essential that we learn to control our emotions while at the same time appreciate them no matter the experience we might be facing.

Anger

To a certain degree there is nothing wrong with feeling angry; in fact, it can be what gets us motivated to make a difference in our lives and that of others. In a sense, anger can encourage us to get involved; it can invoke in us a desire to change, either internally or externally. Whether or not it's beneficial, amounts to how we utilize our feelings of anger and the effects it has on us as a result.

While I like to point out the positives of the whole spectrum of emotions we experience, there is, of course, the downside. While some can channel their anger into positive goals, this is not an option for everyone, whether it's due to the circumstances for their anger or an inability to harness it. The presence of occasional anger is a perfectly normal and healthy response; it would be an issue within itself if someone didn't have a negative reaction to certain situations, such as a miscarriage of justice. However, living in a perpetual state of anger is an unhealthy choice and in some cases the person in question may not even be aware of it. For instance, some project their anger and hate onto others rather than searching internally to discover the emotions they harbor and why it's affecting them so profoundly. This is not an uncommon situation and it can readily be identified in many bullies, which is an ever-growing topic of concern. We encounter such people every day, whether it's the occasional road rage, the impossible-to-please boss, and even ourselves. It's easy to simply write these people off as jerks and leave it at that, but it's important to remember that anger grows from something deeper, often starting as a seed of hurt or pain. When we look at these people through a window of compassion we are more readily to recognize and turn it onto ourselves, and to take a pause so that we can be objective rather than take it personally and lash out onto others.

Dealing with the repeated rise of anger within oneself can be made all that much more difficult if one was not taught how to cope with such intense feelings. Unfortunately, this missing link often goes hand in hand with being raised in inhospitable environments, creating feelings of resentment, inadequacies, and rejection, just to name a few. These emotions aren't just sparked in the home, but also amongst our peers who we may feel alienated or persecuted by. Perhaps worse than not possessing any coping skills, is being taught destructive emotional responses from a young age, such as associating kindness with weakness or shame in crying and expression.

In the absence of emotional education, our incapacity inevitably follows us into adulthood and our relationships. Depending on the root of one's anger, a person's behavior can display itself in a multitude of ways. Perhaps it manifests itself in a constant state of antagonism over the most insignificant of events or maybe it's fueled by a need to control and dominate, often seen in abusive relationships with both partners and children. This misguided expression against others stems from something; hostility is not exhibited without cause. Anger is not limited to being projected onto others but can also be directed towards ourselves. In some instances, we are actively taught to hate ourselves by either family or peers and in others it may be a byproduct of being disappointed in one's own actions. The consequences for our anger is contingent upon the reasoning behind it, and can range anywhere between schoolyard bullying, (which we are realizing more and more can be incredibly cruel and therefore have dangerous repercussions), self-harm, and domestic abuse. As I state repeatedly throughout this book, it's imperative to identify the source. We cannot hope to break our destructive cycles without knowing why we are inclined to act in the manner we do.

Ask yourself if you have an unhealthy relationship with anger. For many of you the extremes of this emotion will not be applicable, so you may be prepared to dismiss the possibility.

- However, are there any topics or actions that inspire a reaction that from an outside perspective might be considered an irrational response?

_____
_____
_____
_____
_____

- For those who do experience the reality of un-abating anger, are you aware of the cause?

_____

_____

_____

_____

_____

- If not, perhaps make a list of what sparks your temper and see if there is a common factor.

_____

_____

_____

_____

_____

Fear & Stress

In the pursuit of our goals we inevitably face obstacles that either hinder or stop us in our tracks; it's unfortunate and all the more debilitating that two such factors often resonate from ourselves. I'm talking about fear and stress. Both of which have personally been a barrier in my past and still crop up today. Their influence becomes all the more noteworthy as one generally correlates to the other. Our fears increase our stress level and an overload of stress ignites our nerves and fears along with it, quickly forming an endless spiral that overtakes us. In the normal sporadic event fear and stress are linked to the fight and flight response meant to alert us in times of trouble, however, as times have changed, so has our state of being.

We all have goals in life, whether it's something seemingly small like losing weight or more challenging like overcoming an addiction. Embarking on a new path is both an exciting and fearful prospect. For some, even making the decision to begin can appear and feel intimidating. Many of us wave off the idea of change as unnecessary or a waste of time without questioning why we are doing so in the first place. Moreover, we might altogether stray from attempting to pinpoint or much less take under consideration if there might be an underlying reason that something is holding us back. Fear of failure, change, the unknown, and even success can prevent us from accomplishing what we aspire towards. However, in allowing it that power we are also impeding our opportunity to discover our limits and capabilities which is an injustice to our person. If we take that leap we may end up surprising ourselves.

The cloud of fear that inhibits us, is just another facet of stress that we encounter on a daily basis. Often undermined and not given nearly enough credence by many, is the factor that stress plays into our daily routine, moods, health, and success. Just as the definition implies, the sheer strain stress exerts on our lives and mental being is overwhelming. In fact, stress is said to be considered the number one factor of most of our illnesses, both mental and physical. During my sister's illness, I read countless information regarding cancer, trying to get a deeper understanding to what was happening to her. Throughout my studies, stress and fear were mentioned time and time again; it appeared to be a pivotal factor in many of our current critical health issues, recognized by many physicians, clinicians, and analysts.

Robert Morris Sapolsky[3], a professor in neurological science, at Stanford University lectures on our various mental states and explains how fear and stress have become our personal killers. In his fantastic documentary, National Geographic: *Stress: Portrait of a Killer*, Sapolsky lays out the way our bodies and chemistry react to stress; it is incredibly insightful and available for purchase on Amazon.

---

[3]   https://www.youtube.com/user/StanfordUniversity/search?query=sapolsky

Prevailing over these hurdles in search of personal growth may require a bit more work but it makes it no less worthwhile. Stress has always been particularly onerous for me and was responsible for my escape in alcohol. When it comes to fear, I've found that boosting confidence fortifies a person's resolve. Make a list of your accomplishments; this isn't limited to financial or social success as society's perception dominates. This small task will have a varying degree of difficulty depending on each individual's situation. Begin by setting small goals for yourself and increasing your ambition as you accomplish each one.

Handling stress is a more subjective topic, as its sources differ so greatly from person to person and therefore, so too do the methods of coping that are both available and work. The average person has a seemingly endless array of responsibilities. The combination of commuting, work, parenting, bills, familial obligations, managing the household, errands, and at times working more than one job can make any day feel like an uphill climb. Introducing new habits and behaviors in the midst of the overwhelming chaos of life is no easy feat. I can empathize with the struggle of the exhausting maintenance of day-to-day life and this is where prioritizing becomes necessary. Don't hold yourself to such high standards that you become burnt out from everyday life; adjust your agenda according to your priorities and take the time to seek outlets and take care of yourself. Many suggest, exercise, a hobby, or simply time management. I know that exercise is often either over emphasized or downplayed, I did the latter for years; however, it really is a crucial means to keep us not only healthy, but to release the heavy burdens we place on ourselves. For one, it takes you away from your current state of mind, and two, it relieves the body of the built-up tension. Physically you may feel exhausted following your workout, but it also infiltrates one's mental energy, sparking the desire to move forward.

Proper stress management is crucial, especially for those of us who are easily overwhelmed. I remember being told "Don't Sweat the Small Stuff", but until I read the book by Richard Carlson[4] I was more likely to do just that. It is so easy to allow minor things to take hold, and I am sure my depression and alcoholism played a factor. There are endless components that play a role in how we wake up and face our day, but stress and fear shouldn't be the dominating ones. To be ruled by these inhibitors is nothing less than a waste of our time. We can't predict with certainty that what we fear and stress over will come to fruition. We can merely hope to face it with calm and grace if it does come to pass, an act that would be all the more difficult if we have been bogged down by the pressure of anticipation. The best course of action is to make the most of our time, by not squandering precious time, energy, and health on needless worry.

What I have learned from both Richard Carlson's book and Robert Sapolsky's lectures, is something that may come across as common sense, yet most of us do not live by this

---

[4]   https://www.amazon.com/dp/B000FC1VX8/ref=dp-kindle-redirect?_encoding=UTF8&btkr=1

ideology, regrettably allowing these influences to defeat us. It's time to take action and decide that you can control your life's pursuit once you take the reins and decide that you won't tolerate its constraint!

The point is, take that step to search for what will both relieve your emotional and mental burdens and yet still allow you to manage daily life. Also know that there's no shame in asking for help, much less in putting yourself first when it comes to your health, whether it's physical or mental.[5] After all, the better state of health, be it mind, body, or spirit, only makes it easier when having to face a tough ordeal or crisis and in being able to care for your loved ones in their time of need.

- Let's take a moment for some self-reflection. Do you harbor any doubts or fears that stop you from pursuing new goals or pursuits?

_____

_____

_____

_____

_____

---

[5]   On that note, YouTube has many powerful motivational speeches that are available to watch all for free https://www.youtube.com/user/HayHousePresents
https://www.youtube.com/user/BrendonBurchard and https://www.youtube.com/user/TheChopraWell just to name but a few.

- What are some of the stressors and fears you encounter frequently?

_____

_____

_____

_____

_____

- Do you feel they have influenced your health? If so, what adjustments can you incorporate to temper or alleviate them?

_____

_____

_____

_____

_____

$\mathcal{S}adness$

Feeling sadness is a normal part of life; there are moments in each of our lives that we are going to feel sad, whether it's due to a break-up, job loss, harsh words, or a tragic event. And sometimes it just hits you out of the blue, perhaps triggered by a familiar song, the emotion just seeps out from inside us. In these moments I just break down in tears; a rush comes through me and I cry hard and loud, various upsetting memories run through my mind as I allow the pain to run its course and eventually subside. Naturally these occurrences fill me with heartache, but when I'm crying over lost loved ones, for example, I also feel as though I'm sharing with them my love and support. As I see it - it's a way of honoring them, remembering them, and even asking for their forgiveness as I have made plenty of mistakes.

Moreover, when I allow this massive storm of emotions filled with tears and sobs to explode from my inner being, I inevitably feel free in the aftermath. The concept of finding liberation through expression is hardly a new one and yet so many of us are still reluctant to expose ourselves, especially for those who were raised to expect scorn or belittlement for expressing our emotions. Holding so tightly to things that trouble us, even the seemingly trivial, only make our perceptions of circumstances seem more dire than they are.

Carrying a heavier weight is the feeling of despair, I recall distinctly my loss of hope and faith, and questioning the reasoning behind my presence on this earth. Despair is likely to be correlated to the circumstances we find ourselves in, be it an unhealthy/abusive marriage, death of a loved one, or a traumatic experience. These types of events can be catastrophic to our overall health and understandably so. It at times feels like these instances are cropping up more now than ever before, such as the tragedies of the Pulse nightclub or Parkland shootings. As a result, we are also more aware of and accepting of the toll it takes on a person's mental state, such as PTSD, than we ever have been in the past. The condition having long been ignored and downplayed for years, much like depression, which I'll expand on shortly.

As previously mentioned, disappointment and sorrow are a natural state to experience in day-to-day life; it's when there's a significant shift in the balance of our emotions, that there's an issue. The reasons behind the unhealthy tip of the scale can range from mental illness, such as depression, to being plagued by demons from the past. Regardless, dwelling over our circumstances is debilitating and prevents us from fulfilling our goals; therefore, these pains that are stalling our forward movement in life, need to be addressed.

In so far as depression, I speak of it only as it is related to me. I am not here to give advice, as I am not a licensed psychiatrist. This is solely my experience regarding depression. Depression can manifest itself differently in others, but if you find yourself discovering parallels between your and my experience, perhaps you might like to investigate it more with a professional.

Throughout my years of being plagued with depression, a chorus of questions would bombard my mind. I often wondered why me, why was I here on this earth? I asked this question to myself countless times and made note that if there was such a thing as reincarnation that I never wanted to come back here again; this place was not for me. I would think to myself, who was I? And why did I have to know myself?

Eventually, I would learn this is a common occurrence and feeling in many people's lives. During conversations with others, who were also in a state of depression, I heard this same sentiment; they felt the same uncertainty that I did. During my continuous research of depression over the years, my studies have shown repeated claims that people who are depressed have a low frequency level; I, however, have a very different theory and it is simply from a message that has come to me time and time again. That message has instead solidified my belief that our frequency levels are not low at all, but rather in tune with the world around us and all its corruption, injustices, and catastrophes. In effect, this strong pulsation tends to overshadow our positive vibrations, often causing us to retreat and even to an extent paralyze us. This paralysis is why we have been misconstrued as lazy, and the dogmatic stigma has only furthered people to withdraw and isolate themselves in defense.

Despite appearances, behind the scenes, our minds are far from inactive but rather either running restlessly with ruminating thoughts or burdened by a barrage of negativity, effectively weighing us down. It's my opinion, that for those of us who have suffered with depression, this vibrational signal we are receiving is one that is instead meant to spur us forward to pursue our true purpose. I have always believed this deep down. This belief was further encouraged by an article in the New York Times Magazine, *Depression's Upside* by J. Anderson Thomson, Jr., M.D., a psychiatrist who correlates the connection to a wakeup call. A very interesting study and worthwhile read.[6]

I was raised very fortunate, at least materially, from a young age. I considered it a great upbringing until the age of 12 when my depression set in. I could never say why or where it originated; was it hereditary (from my father), my menstrual cycle, binge drinking, or the drastic changes in my lifestyle. Nonetheless, prior to this onset I was a very enthusiastic young girl from what I remember; my sister even wrote a poem to the whole family, matching us to a tee, stating that I was "lost in my imagination, no reality." I lived in the state of imagination until I discovered the real world that existed. I was indeed one privileged girl, yet I am afraid once I came to the realization that the world I knew, was nothing like that of the one that really existed, things changed for me. And to a degree it debilitated me and made my depression even stronger, that is until I decided to change the way I looked at life.

---

[6]   For more information you can visit his website. http://www. jandersonthomson.com/

Later in life I learned just how much my drinking exacerbated my depression; it truly made it ten times more debilitating. I would contemplate suicide over the most trivial issues that transpired. Since becoming sober, my depression has dramatically altered; of course, it did not magically dissipate but it has made the effects of drinking all the more apparent. Before, minor occurrences would set me off course for weeks, often beginning with a negative thought that would quickly encompass my entire outlook on anything and everything. Ruminating thoughts would consume me, continuously reviewing every bad choice I'd ever made or all the injustices in society. I would lose any positive countenance I possessed and the only escape in sight would be alcohol. While I tricked myself into believing it was a balm for my pain, it never truly offered any relief. Immediately following my indulgence, the ruminating thoughts only worsened, capitalized by the guilt and sense of failure that accompanied my choice to drink, inevitably leading to weeks of depression and the struggle to just get out of bed.

While sobriety did a world of good in shifting my depressive states, it also came down to recognizing the signs and progression of my particular circumstances. I came to correlate my bouts of depression with a lack of coping skills. Typically, it begins with becoming overwhelmed, which for me had a history of occurring with even the most insignificant of things. The phrase making a mountain out of a molehill does not fully emphasize how easily and profoundly I could be affected. Next, the task or situation at hand would color everything else in a film of negativity; it's truly as if I were looking through a different set of lenses, geared only towards a defeatist outlook. Since becoming more familiar with the pattern of my depression, I've been able to manage it better. For instance, one morning I decided to work on a landscaping project in my backyard. But almost immediately after stepping outside I became overwhelmed by the project, and my penchant for perfectionism made it appear all the more challenging. I turned heel back inside to have some coffee and take a deeper look into my mindset, acknowledging that this was a situation that would normally be a foothold for a depressive state. I told myself that this was exactly my problem, I allow myself to get too emotional over things. Instead I ignored the negativity that was pulsing through my being and forced myself to get to work, repeating positive affirmations as I did so. I can't say that I am successful every time, but my awareness and sobriety has made a remarkable change in my depression and the means in which I handle it.

Joy & Gratitude

William Blake stated, *"A fool sees not the same tree that a wise man sees."*[7]

While there may be many ways in which to interpret this famous quote, for me it tells me that our perception of life is fundamental to our life's journey. That is to say, that we hold the choice in how we perceive life, such as seeing the glass half empty or half full. However, this perception can be altered at any time we choose to do so. For far too often we hear only of the bad and this becomes too controlling, provoking us to live in fear which, as previously mentioned, is disabling. For this reason alone, we should take careful time and energy to remind ourselves of what in life we do have to be appreciative of. To take time every day, to ponder over all the things we are thankful for. In doing so, we not only raise ourselves up, but it may eventually serve as a step in making a difference for others.

There are many things we love and hold dear in life, whether it's the people in our lives, precious memories, aspirations we seek, or even nature itself and all the wonders of this astounding life that unfolds before us. If we let them, these joys we encounter can embolden us to set forth in our

---

[7] Copyright © 2018 William Blake Archive. Used with permission.

ambitions, make us feel vibrant, and truly blessed. These are the feelings we would wish to have on a daily basis, that encourage us to live in the moment and give us the motivation to forge ahead on our path to change and fulfillment of life.

Even when the moment seems bleak, there is always something in life to be grateful for. This gratitude, reassures us, makes us mindful and is essential when it comes to living a life dedicated to our health and happiness. In order to harness it, we ought to make note of our good experiences so that we have them as a constant reminder. Yet, to both obtain and maintain these positive emotions, still requires a foray into the, at times, brutal and painstaking truth found along the path of forgiveness.

All too often we lose sight of the joy in life and become bogged down with daily stressors. When that negative shift in our perspective occurs, we need to refocus on what uplifts us. So, take a moment to list what brings you happiness and what you are grateful for.

_____

_____

_____

_____

_____

Honesty

The final two pivotal factors are honesty and forgiveness. Many relationship teachings find that it is crucial to have open and honest talks with one another. This type of dialogue is not as prevalent as it should be. Still, if we want to have a true relationship with a partner, family member, our children, or friends, we need to not only be able to express our true feelings to them, but to also reciprocate in receiving their message to us as well. And it usually sets out with the person telling the other, "When you do this or that, this is how it makes me feel." When you know that something you are doing is hurting someone you love, then attempting to change that behavior should matter.

Of course, changing one's behavior is not always an easy task, but the first step is being open to feedback. So, if a loved one comes to you and expresses themselves, take the time to understand where their message is coming from, even if it's critical in nature. We can't grow in life if we are immediately on the defensive. Listen, don't just react, to what is being said from an objective point of view. If then you feel your loved one is making a valid point, you can make note of the issue and attempt to change the behavior, one step at a time.

For a more lighthearted example, my daughter once relayed to me that I constantly speak about negative things right before bedtime. It had never occurred to me but, she was right. Why on earth could I spend all day in such a positive mood, then right before bed begin thinking of the horrors of the world and speak with her about it to boot! Well, watching the evening news might have had something to do with it, but caring for her feelings was much more important so I had to change this habit. I knew I might not always be mindful of this change, therefore I made note of it on my refrigerator and read it several times a day until I no longer behaved in that fashion; no longer watching the news at night, of course, had a helpful impact on my mindset, hers included.

Inadvertently, we all do things that others may find hurtful or troublesome, often times unknowingly; but if we are open to feedback and expressions of honesty, we can begin to make changes. However, there are always those who immediately respond defensively, perceiving any approach to sensitive topics as an insult. When we encounter these individuals in life, it makes having a healthy and honest relationship difficult, especially if it's a family member.

Personally, I could never have these discussions with my family; for whenever I attempted to speak up, I was usually berated, shunned, and told to quit complaining. For instance, my mother once asked me not to speak about my siblings to her, that it irritated her, and she did not want to be put in the middle; I understood where she was coming from and immediately acquiesced. It was ironic, however, that the very next day when I came to visit she began criticizing my father, as she often did. It had long been an uncomfortable situation for me, especially given my close relationship with my father but I'd always kept quiet, uneasy about speaking up. However, considering my mother's request the day before I felt she'd be receptive if I made the same plea. Instead, the expression of my feelings was interpreted an attack and I was told to leave.

I relay this example just to show how it's not always possible to establish a real connection with those closest to us. We can't create and nurture honest bonds when the other is not willing to meet you halfway. We've all encountered these unequal relationships in our lives and at times deemed them worthwhile and just coped with the imbalance. However, circumstances and dynamics are incredibly subjective from person to person and for some, the cost of familial relationships can be damaging, whether it's upon your physical person, self-esteem, or emotional/mental wellbeing. If you are seeking change in your life, the prospect of cutting ties with loved ones may become a real consideration. I know this to be one of the hardest things to do. I walked away from my family during a very difficult time; but had I not done so, I would not have had the strength to reunite with my parents and to assist them in their time of need, prior to their deaths when the rest of the family were not there for them.

Not everyone is willing to change, and many are not even willing to admit that they could benefit by doing so, refusing to admit to possessing any faults at all. For this very reason, not all relationships are able to be rectified, but being aware of this fact is essential. It may mean that you need to distance yourself from these stubborn individuals or acknowledge that certain relationships will not last.

We must be honest with ourselves if we are to ever live the plentiful life we were meant to. Honesty is something that is often undermined and ridiculed, as if no one is capable of such a feat. Yet, being forthright with oneself about who we are, how we deal with life's endeavors, and how we react to situations that arise is pertinent to pursuing your personal growth The subject of honesty and living by it is not always clear cut as we'd expect. Sometimes there is a difference between what is our truth and that of others. Our perceptions have an integral influence on how we react, think, and live life. We may see something differently than those around us. By living in truth, I mean that you must be completely open and honest with yourself about who you are, your life circumstances, and past tragedies. The truth can be painful to bear and is why most of us avoid it at all costs. Others, have created their truth as their life has unfolded; in which case, the individual may not be able to see things as they truly are.

For those who choose to avoid the discomfort and are reluctant to face bad things they may have done to others, to themselves, or been done to them, this will only hinder one's ability to genuinely heal. It is natural for us to avoid pain, and the majority have no real desire to live in such a state. But not unlike an athlete who undergoes unpleasantness and injuries as they push through that extra mile to grow in their craft, we too must endure the emotional pain to grow as a human being. It is imperative to feel it deeply, allowing it to be released through tears and communication. Being brutally honest about our mistakes may seem intimidating, but if we all were to come forward and admit these misdeeds, soon like everything else, it would become second nature. With time and effort, the suffering will subside; mental and spiritual freedom awaits on the other side of the tumultuous healing process.

• Do you feel you have an honest relationship with others and/or yourself?

_____

_____

_____

_____

_____

• Have you buried any issues you have with your loved ones because you are uncertain of their reception if you spoke out?

_____

_____

_____

_____

_____

- Is there anything you might not be acknowledging? That you have hidden away because you fear the pain if confronted?

_____

_____

_____

_____

_____

- Are you open to feedback from others?

_____

_____

_____

_____

_____

Forgiveness

Being open and honest also means having the ability to forgive. Not only forgiving others but yourself as well. It is often times harder for us to forgive ourselves than it is to forgive others and the effects of carrying that burden are not easily ignored. I truly believe that my sister's cancer arose from her inability to forgive herself. I remember the words she spoke to me and my mother prior to knowing she had cancer throughout her bones; she said, "it is eating me up alive." During a shared meditation she asked me how she could forgive herself. I told her if I could forgive her, she should be able to as well; clearly the reality is not so simple. Isn't it odd, that we are more likely to forgive others, but not ourselves. Why is this? Perhaps it's because we have to live with ourselves and the constant reminders that our minds force us to relive, steered automatically towards negativity. I can easily relate, as for years with my depression I would reevaluate my past mistakes; they haunted me. I found it so painstakingly hard to forgive the mistakes I'd made, even minor petty things, that others had no recollection of when I brought it to their attention to ask for their forgiveness.

So of course, it was easy for me to forgive her, because as an outsider we can gain some distance from the wrongs we didn't commit. Now, I wholeheartedly believe that this is a result of not only our upbringing but society as well, a conditioning that can be altered, over time, for our future generations. Too often our minds hold us captive with thoughts of our past wrongs, unintentionally empowering their control and preventing our ability to forgive. Even what we deny and have purposely turned away from, find ways to make themselves known in one form or another. But it can also be altered in the here and now, if we so choose and that is why it will be very important for you to control your state of mind which will be discussed further in a later chapter.

Another aspect I've observed when it comes to the act of forgiveness, is the ease of applying it to strangers as opposed to those we know. It's likely attributed to the fact that we have less expectations of strangers and the ties we have with loved ones mean the offending act represents a more personal attack than it would coming from someone we don't know. There is also a sense of betrayal involved that has to be overcome in order to forgive, which doesn't exist with an outsider.

Offering forgiveness to others or ourselves does not equate to denying the event in question ever took place or that it doesn't matter, a common fear that also inhibits us from moving forward. It does not mean that you condone a person's actions; it simply allows you to heal and move on by releasing the weight you are encumbered by. Even after I've expressed my apologies and received forgiveness in turn, my wrongs occasionally seep into my thoughts, and while I still acknowledge it today, it does not have the hold on me it did yesterday or the day before that, and so on.

When we refuse to offer forgiveness, we are not gaining a win but rather losing out on a life worth living. We are condemning ourselves to stay frozen. If we lived in a state of mind where being painfully honest was commonplace, we would not face this dilemma and the propaganda of growth would not be as prevalent today. Nevertheless, here we are. It is more common to avoid pain and the truth of who we are, what we have done, and how we have acted or reacted than to face it head on. The result is a life not far from the drama of a soap opera and inevitably ends on a deathbed of regrets. I have seen it too many times, witnessed people near their end, desperately seeking closure and to make amends with their wrong doings. There has to be a latent reason that this is such a common occurrence in us when we reach that pivotal moment in our lives. And if only we did not look at our mistakes so harshly, undermining ourselves in the process, we might not feel the need to hide in shame. *You're Only Human* (by Billy Joel) - Making mistakes is how we learn; it is how we grow. We must learn to forgive ourselves just as we would others that we love.

While no one wants to see their loved ones harmed or even killed, I firmly believe that their loss of life was not in vain. When our loved ones move on, there is a lesson to be learned. One in which we are to come together, be forthcoming with others and ourselves, so that we might find it in our hearts to forgive. To utilize their lives as a means to empower others is a crucial endeavor that in the end is not only freeing and enlightening, but also keeps their memory alive.[8]

- How do you view forgiveness? Do you believe offering it means condoning bad behavior?

_____

_____

_____

_____

_____

- Do you harbor any grudges or resentment?

_____

_____

_____

_____

_____

---

[8]   If the idea of forgiveness is a difficult or unthinkable step for you, I would recommend checking out The Forgiveness Project. Formed and run by both Katy Hutchison and Ryan Aldridge, the man who killed her husband. It's a moving and inspirational story that was made into a Lifetime movie, *Bond of Silence.* http://theforgivenessproject.com/stories/katy-hutchison-ryan-aldridge-canada/

- Have you forgiven others for trespasses against yourself? What were they?

_____

_____

_____

_____

_____

Complaints & Our Reactions

Will Bowen a public speaker and creating founder of the "Complaint Free Movement"[9] came out with the purple wristband, meant to be worn during a 21-day experiment to keep people more self-consciously aware of their constant complaining. His book, *A Complaint Free World*, is both a worthwhile read, as well as, a smart analysis of the means to help people become more aware of our trivial actions that often distract and erode our real-life agenda.

While an insightful project, we should not mis-categorize this as the same for people who really are in need of assistance. The 3-week challenge is an eye-opening memento that can redirect our focus and remind us of all the gratitude we ought to have. And taking time each morning and/or evening to give thanks and acknowledging all we have to be grateful for is an important stride for true growth, as well as keeping us centered and focused.

Just like many people, I have learned, as a once deeply depressed person, to use the losses I have endured as a means to keep myself centered and focused. At this very moment I am looking upon the photos of my departed loved ones, reminded of the fact that they were type A personalities, real go getters,

---

[9] https://www.willbowen.com/complaintfree/

much more so than I. As I write this, I feel deeply that they are still with me, inspiring me with their perpetual ambition, pushing me full steam ahead.

Let us not become distracted. I want you to think for a moment how you begin your day, perhaps at first you wake up in a good mood and then something happens to change that. A driver cuts you off or once you get to work you find out you are not getting that promotion you had been counting on. It could be anything trivial or even crucial to your life that takes place. Are you prepared for this? No one is ever necessarily prepared for bad news or complications, but it is nevertheless a fact of life. I have always justified the bad in life based upon the ideology that without it we would not know the good. However, it is the way we handle the stumbling blocks, that is essential to our life. While we may not have the ability to control what comes our way – we do indeed have control of how we handle it. By allowing the bad to distract and steer us off course, we are essentially giving it the power to dominate us; therefore, we are not truly living our life to its fullest means. What we do possess, however, is the ability to rise to the occasion by not letting it get the best of us. In handling the situation, our decisive decision vs. indecisiveness is the key. The best way in changing our bad habits for the better is one step at a time.

First, we never want to immediately react, but instead respond after careful thought. For the instances in which we deviate from this advice, there is always a lesson to be gained. We've all encountered ridiculous and dangerous drivers on the road, and it can easily get our blood boiling. The smart and safe reaction is to dismiss the driver and the incident, but we don't always take this road. On one occasion, for example, I came across another car driving erratically in the entrance to my neighborhood, causing me to back up and maneuver around his unpredictable driving. My irritation by his bizarre behavior was only enhanced by the fact that I was almost repeatedly hit in an entrance that is unusually large. I immediately reacted by following him around the neighborhood, not the wisest idea. Later I realized I didn't know this person's mentality or how he could have reacted to my pursuit, so I wrote a note to myself, Safety First and Foremost. Not only did I react without thinking but I also allowed my irritation with his unsafe driving to follow me throughout my day, throwing me entirely off my agenda. In the end my actions were not worth the risk. As someone who has struggled with the inability to deal with bad shit as it comes, I, like many people, tend to allow it to rule me.

It was the main cause for my drinking, allowing any little pivotal issues that arose to influence my desire to escape and thus drink as a means to do so. So now I attempt to remind myself of this every day before interacting with others or leaving my home, Safety First and Foremost. I do not know what is happening in another person's life, they too could be having a bad day; be nice, show them kindness, do not allow their bad behavior to affect you. It can be all too easy to forget this approach, especially for those of us who are prone to overreacting, as we are more than familiar with the ease of getting off track and losing sight of control when faced with issues that may or may not be inconsequential.

For those who are afflicted with a runaway train of negative thoughts, finding a way to halt them is imperative to a healthy mindset. Attempting to mitigate our thoughts just proves the importance of living in the moment, always aware of yourself to retain control over your feelings, thoughts, and reactions when confronted with the bad. Moreover, there is something to be learned from the unfavorable experiences that we face. To me, the most crucial lesson of life, is realizing how easy it is for us to get swept up and defeated by all the bad things that we eventually allow to govern us, consequently missing the teachable moments that could have been. I look at the loss of my loved ones, as a means to fulfill a goal; a goal that I believe they internalized, that through me will be fulfilled. Therefore, I now choose not to become sidetracked by complaining. I have much to be thankful for, and for all the bad that is taking place, I plan to find ways to do my part in helping out. All of the real complaints society has will be further discussed in my next upcoming book.

- Take the time to list all the complaints and negative thoughts you have on a typical day. Then do the same with your positive thoughts and thanks.

_____

_____

_____

_____

_____

- If you discover a substantial imbalance, how exactly do you think that influences your general behavior? Does it inspire you to revise your mental approach?

_____

_____

_____

_____

_____

- List what has gone wrong for you this past week/ month.

_____

_____

_____

_____

_____

- How did you handle these experiences, if at all? Was it healthy?

_____

_____

_____

_____

_____

• Would you use the same method today?

_____

_____

_____

_____

_____

Ego

Freud saw the human psyche as three dimensional, ranging from the id, ego, and the superego. The id is considered hereditary, created from birth and as such is part of our subconscious self; whereas the superego usually sets in around the age of three and continues to grow over time and is based upon our environmental surroundings. Meeting in the center is the ego itself, that attempts to mediate both the id and the superego. Once again, we see the antithesis in our lives, which furthers the importance of finding the middle ground. Our ego often gets in our way as I know it did in my family; the need to be right was so critical it dominated all else.

Eckhart Tolle also speaks in regard to overcoming the ego and the difference of acknowledging that being proud of something might be okay but favoring your pride and failing to be humble is not only egotistical, it often overshadows our deeper connections. Our superego often gets in our way, and in many cases leads us on a life path that separates us from others and could be a potential cause for a person's emotional detachment from others, such as a Narcissistic personality disorder.[10] A person's ego may have developed a need for

---

[10] Lisa A. Romano Breakthrough Life Coach℠ & Author https://www.lisaaromano.com/

control, power, and abuse. More than likely the superego is so powerful because inside the person may feel rather empty, they are missing something and longing for it, but do not and will not acknowledge it, for it is viewed as a sign of weakness.

Sadly, this lack of acknowledgement is exactly what holds them back and keeps them weak when on the outside they think they look strong and powerful. Making it critical for anyone who wants to truly awaken and regain control over one's life, is the need to be brutally honest and upfront with any inner demons that have been kept hidden away, because most of our systematic way of life stems from our past. While there is still a lot of controversy over those who lack empathy and their ability to regain it at a later time in life, I truly believe that anything can be overcome once a person is both willing and ready to confront the past, which brought them to where they find themselves today.

The "need to be right" happens to be a very crucial factor in our interactions with others. Admitting to one's wrongs is hard for many to come to terms with and the refusal to do so can resemble something not unlike an addiction. This mindset can become so persistent that denial becomes a natural reaction. The stubborn stance that one is never wrong undoubtedly creates a rift, not only in our relationships but within ourselves, preventing us from seeing the truth. Living by this creed will put a stop to any attempt for genuine growth, as it can't be attained without honesty. The origins of a mentality that needs to be right can develop from any number of things, insecurity, perfectionism, or perhaps a spoiled childhood. If there's been a pattern that points to this attitude or you suspect you have this tendency, don't dismiss it. Don't trivialize the affect it can have on your relationships. Whether it's a casual conversation or a serious addressment of an issue, being on the receiving end of an individual who always needs to be right puts a serious strain on how we view and feel about that person. Thus, if you want to maintain your meaningful relationships, it's necessary to set aside your ego.

In more extreme cases the surety of our position can extend beyond obstinate disagreement to imposing our belief on others. Take for instance the dynamics within a family with opposing beliefs on LGBT[11] views, such as between parent and child. Countless instances of pressuring conformity have led to either obliging to the parent's ego and therefore living an unhappy life or even worse, such as suicide.

Remember that it really is okay to be wrong. We cannot be right all the time and in everything. What is the point of learning and true growth if we are stuck in the belief that it is our way or the highway? After all, when we look out into this marvelous world of ours we see nothing but diversity and the phenomenal variety of paths it offers, how can we be so obstinate that there is only one way or point of view?

"To be yourself in a world that is constantly trying to make you something else is the greatest accomplishment." Ralph Waldo Emerson

---

[11]   LGBT National Help Center: https://www.glbthotline.org/

- Do you think you allow your behavior to be ruled by your ego?

_____

_____

_____

_____

_____

- Do you or anyone you know, have a persisting need to be right?

_____

_____

_____

_____

_____

- If you have this tendency, where do you believe it originates from?

_____

_____

_____

_____

_____

CHAPTER 3

True Growth

The message of this chapter was a source of inspiration for me in writing this book, but it may also be considered the more difficult path. Obviously, the process of changing one's life is no simple task, otherwise we'd be observing a world far different than the one that exists. From a basic perspective, it is humanity's default to become accustomed to our life's patterns from the moment of birth. We can also contend that this conditioning does not occur solely within the family unit, but also through society's social network of ideology, which subtly dominates our existence. One such stance, that permeates a significant percentage of the population's mindset, is the idea that acknowledging how our circumstances of the past have influenced our present, is considered a sign of weakness.

As countless others, I too, grew up in a family that regarded harboring over past problems as a defect or a cop out. There's a stigma that continues to persist today, surrounding the revisiting of our childhood; many would write these individuals off, claiming they merely seek a platform for their "poor me" story. Yes, it is damaging to stay stuck in the past, but it is just as detrimental to bury pain and trials. Honest confrontation with one's self is the gateway to True Growth.

Not only is a personal quest a prerequisite for changing one's self and life, but it can serve as training for how to approach future struggles in a way that is best for you. And perhaps what we learn can be passed onto others.

While many motivational speakers relay the importance of being present in the Now moment, there's a difference between those who are truly at peace and those who have swept things under the rug. For those who have chosen the latter, whether they are aware or not, our past has a tendency to resurface in unexpected and inconvenient ways. Regardless of how it manifests itself, the fact that we can be negatively influenced by our history, makes the task of facing it a strength, not a weakness. If you want to be free of pain, fear, hate, self-destruction, anger, depression, addictions, and any other self-destructive knots, you need to commit to the, oftentimes, difficult road of facing old demons.

We've all heard it before, but it is very common for victims of abuse to develop relationships with figures similar to their abusers. On the outside looking in, we ask ourselves why these people would continue such an obvious destructive pattern. But on the inside, the situation is not so easily separated into terms of right and wrong, as the mind is so twistedly conditioned that the individual is compelled to seek only what they know. Freud termed this pattern the Repetition Compulsion. While his beliefs as to why people repeat patterns, even if it is not in their best interest, may differ from my own and others, it does not change the fact that from infanthood, we tend to cling to behavioral routines. Even if it's traumatic, we are prone to replicate them in other areas of life.

This concept really hit home for me while attending a Joyce Myers event years ago, with my mother and daughter. She told a story of an eagle's circular flight and how it mirrored our actions. She asserted that until we stop avoiding our issues, God will ensure we'll continue to be confronted by the same situations we want to escape. Her message behind the story differed from Freud's clinical view, but both raise relatable questions about the patterns we fall into.

Sadly, due to inattention and not living in the present moment, we continue to perpetuate these patterns. When faced with the inevitable self-pity and defeatism that follows this behavior, the prospect of escaping the cycle may not even touch one's mind. If and when we have come to this place in life, it's imperative to take control of your thinking patterns. Painful though it may be, take a good, hard, and honest in-depth look into your life and your past. This may mean confronting past mistakes and hard truths, but it will also shine a light on the reasoning for your present state. The prospect of admitting to past mistakes may be misconstrued as a form of disparaging one's self, serving as a deterrent. But the truth is that self-awareness is a necessary step in the gateway towards self-acceptance and discovering one's self-worth.

Following self-enlightenment, shedding negativity and becoming unstuck is still a trying task, despite having an awareness for why we make the decisions that we do. In the midst of self-discovery, life and all its curveballs will continue to come at you. For some, these situations are more dominating, making the steps we know we need to take all the more arduous. While a reprieve from the stressors of life would be ideal when working on one's self and striving for such a drastic change, it's not an option for the majority of us. Struggling to maintain a path towards change becomes more compounded by the fact that we also become comfortable with the disconnect and chaos in our lives, so much so, that we end up fearing that if something good happens, something bad will shortly follow.

This latter concept can sound insane, that we as humans grow so accustomed to the bad, that we come to depend on it and its twisted reliability. We eventually grow accustomed to our uncomfortable and unfulfilling position in life until it becomes our natural state of being. This dependence on discord also alters our perceptions and outlook on life, forming a mindset that readily sees despair and little hope. Worse yet, due in part to the repetition, some inevitably believe it's deserved. Despite the dangers of this view, it becomes a comfort zone, so much so that escaping the bad can actually make one feel lost. This distorted mindset explains why one would continue down an unhealthy and unjust path in life; not because we necessarily want to, but because it is what we know and so we have grown complacent. We lose sight of what is good and bad, or even just what normal behavior is, becoming disconnected from those around us.

Our detrimental thoughts are not always unhealthy solely for the person in question, but they extend to the friends and family around us and in some cases even further. In his book *Anger, Madness, and the Daimonic*,[12] Dr. Stephen A. Diamond discusses the idea of how these unacknowledged feelings of ours are destructive not just to ourselves, and those we love, but towards society as a whole, and we are seeing this implemented in situations like the mass murders that are taking place. As of recently, some of the news channels are refusing to say the names of the people who have committed these awful crimes. While I will delve into this subject matter more in my next book, I just want to make note that not saying their name does nothing to lend aid in preventing the next event from occurring. For eventually their name will become public knowledge and it is not that we want to promote them or their horrific deeds. However, the only real way to introduce change is by examining them, so that we can apply that knowledge in the future for the pursuit of prevention; for ignoring their existence accomplishes nothing of substance.

Our patterns of self-destructive behaviors are generally linked to past trauma. Though the prospect of sharing our history is an uncomfortable one, it's necessary for growth and an opportunity to aid others. The idea of passing on our messages of our personal stories, which we have overcome, is at times mistakenly regarded as an indulgence for self-pity. However, it is a means to not only connect with others by way of encouragement but reinforces one's own convictions. In

---

[12]   https://www.amazon.com/Anger-Madness-Daimonic-Paradoxical-Creativity-ebook/dp/B00BGVT3KK
       http://psychology.com/

turn, it also serves as a lesson to others and ourselves against repeating the past and its harmful consequences. Sharing that information allows for a deeper insight into our past circumstances and that of others, which adds another layer of protection in combatting future instances that arise to challenge our determination and in doing so we lend the benefits of our experience with others who face similar struggles.

Contrary to the stigma of shame that surrounds the expression of past failure, abuse, mistakes etc., we both crave and benefit from hearing and relating to others' experiences. Take for instance the person responsible for my publishing this book. It is said that when Louise Hay found out she had cancer, she correlated her illness with her inability to truly deal with her childhood abuse. Deciding she would utilize self-healing and forgiveness, she was cured. I myself completely see this as truth and believe in the ideology that we must first change ourselves prior to being of service to others. There is an old poem that comes to mind by an unknown author, possibly a Monk dating back to 1100 A.D.

I Wanted to Change the World

"When I was a young man, I wanted to change the world.
I found it was difficult to change the world, so I tried to change my
nation.
When I found I couldn't change the nation, I began to focus on my
town. I couldn't change the town and as an older man, I tried to
change my family.
Now, as an old man, I realize the only thing I can change is myself,
and suddenly I realize that if long ago I had changed myself, I

could have made an impact on my family. My family and I could
have made an impact on our town. Their impact could have
changed the nation and I could indeed have changed the world."

This poignant poem is applicable to a vast majority of us, because we so deeply want current events and life's circumstances to change, yet many of us deviate, become stuck, or focus on others or outside philosophy and we lose sight of our own divine path. And some of us have just given up. One reason for this is our unwillingness to reflect on who we are and what has shaped us. As previously stated, a great deal of the self-help books and motivational speakers of which I have read along the years tend to ignore past ordeals and instead focus on the present. And although I agree with their perspective on the importance that it is necessary to not stay stuck in the past, the idea of ignoring our past does not and will not - make it go away. We are taught history lessons in school for a reason, so why would we think that our own history should just be ignored?

Most of today's top speakers implore us to get over the past, however, wherever it is you find yourself today, came from your past experiences. Therefore, ignoring them will not change anything; facing them head on is the only true way to move forward in one's life. Accordingly, we begin by learning how to heal those old wounds, come to terms with them, understanding them from a more objective standpoint so that we can move onward towards our true destiny and not chance repeating old patterns out of habit.

- Could there be patterns or self-destructive behaviors that you keep repeating that you have been unaware of? If so, take a moment to think this through and jot them down.

_____
_____
_____
_____
_____

- Or maybe you are aware of them and just not sure how to change?

_____
_____
_____
_____
_____

- Do you have an idea of what produced these patterns?

_____
_____
_____
_____
_____

- Do you believe you deserve happiness and success?

_____

_____

_____

_____

_____

Dealing With The Past

"We repeat what we don't repair." Christine Langley-Obaugh

True growth first begins with being able to get over our past traumas. It is not until we confront these issues head on, that we can live life pursuing our real purpose. I want to emphasize how important I believe this to be. For far too long, many of us have been told to get over it already, build a bridge, or even those with good intentions tell us to focus on the present and that confronting our past demons only keeps us stuck in it.

But I am here to say, this cannot be further from the truth. For we will never move forward, until we have healed those wounds that have influenced our present state. After all, this type of belief often leads people to self-blaming and, at times, re-victimization, which consequently diminishes a person's ability to heal and grow. It is also more often, than not, the cause of our addictions. Being unable to express or confront our past trauma, either due to shame or lack of proper assistance, means it will manifest itself in unhealthy ways. The consequences aren't limited to the typical drug and alcohol addictions but also reveal themselves in eating disorders, hoarding compulsions, self-destructive tendencies and relationship handicaps, just to name a few.

Given this credence, it is essential for you to find the right approach in how to heal, forgive, and thus move forward. Typically, us humans tend to bury wounds of our past in fear of the pain that will ensue from acknowledgment and confrontation. By denying our past and the impact it has undoubtedly had, we are cutting off a fundamental basis of our person and, in a way, not living life fully conscious as our true self. The bypassing of our past and the scars left behind prevents honest healing and the pursuit for the potential we are capable of when not hindered by our trials.

There are many ways in which people deviate around the truth and it is not always intentional, but still harmful. Ignoring painful truths has become a common requisite, something deeply rooted in our culture and not just our own. Our social construct can be partly to blame for this; based upon our beliefs and what we are taught, it no doubt begins from the moment we enter this world of ours and continues because of our desire to fit in and be accepted.

For generations, women and men have hid the secret of being psychically, mentally, and sexually assaulted for either the means of survival or from fear of shame, abandonment, or rejection. Of course, we do not want these disappointments to rule us and there are a variety of ways in which we hide from our inner demons. For some, it is the defensive approach, utilizing rationalization, and repressing to keep the disturbance at bay. We defend ourselves from the truth so that we don't have to readily admit or deal with shame or guilt; instead, we employ forms of denial under the guise of justification. In doing so, we trick ourselves into believing we have moved on but for so many the evidence creeps back in the cycles we repeat, eventually losing sight of the concealed catalyst. Others take a more offensive stance to keep their distress at a distance by way of displacement and projection. The method of displacement is a common theme among those who are abusive, taking out their frustrations on others, often triggered by someone undermining them and used to deviate from their own internal flaws by taking it out on another instead.

Our displacement is also associated with our projecting, meaning we place others at fault instead of identifying the truth about ourselves. Not unlike those who repeatedly seek out abusive relationships, the abuser is also stuck in a cycle. Until the individual acknowledges the source of their actions, the chances of this person being abusive to those they are supposed to love and care about will more than likely become a recurring factor.

Many psychologists, such as Stephen A. Diamond, Ph.D., have suggested that our inner child is still present and is seeking to fix our past. Unconsciously, that child is controlling our present moment, our thoughts, our decisions and as such will seek to find someone similar to that of whomever it was we had conflict with. We unknowingly look for and seek out someone with similar characteristics and traits of the person we long to have loved us. Unless we are truly aware of ourselves and are present in the moment, it is our inner child that is running the show. All the while unaware of our motivations, we misguidedly attempt to heal our wounds by forming relationships with people who share similarities to those who caused them in the first place. We cling to the hope that this time will be different, and we will finally receive what was deprived, whether it's unconditional love, validation, or something else. Dr. Diamond refers to this as a "blind spot," something we are not readily in tune with but is nevertheless fueling our choices in life. During my own path to self-discovery, I found that many of my interactions were driven by my inner child's need for nurturing. After analyzing my actions and feelings, I observed a pattern that surrounded the need to be understood and accepted and it wasn't until I'd recognized this pattern that I fully acknowledged the emotional neglect of my childhood. The realization that a part of our subconscious could influence our behavior to such a degree without even being aware of its origins was a disturbing thought.

While there are many other ways in which we might deviate and cope with our past, I am not a psychiatrist and as such cannot delve into the extensive processes of the mind. I can only implore you to seek enlightenment in areas that are pertinent to your specific situation and share your findings with your loved ones for much needed support or others with similar struggles.

As I mentioned previously in my writing, it can be therapeutic to share and help others but not everyone is willing to make the change.[13] Do not allow others to stifle you from your progress and pursuing your goals in life. We can only spread our knowledge in the hope that others might pay attention, but we cannot force them, nor become deterred from our own path to growth. Remember the poem by the Monk. Begin with you; change starts with one and then spreads to the many.

- Take a moment to write down any hardships you have faced, both past and present.

_____

_____

_____

_____

_____

---

[13] Fortunately, there is more access to self-help these days than there has been in the past, such as local meeting groups, life coaching, and with technology, of course, many online groups and assistance such as: https://www.betterhelp.com/ https://get.talkspace.com/official-site-v2/ https://www.stressreductionspot.com/ https://www.psychologytoday.com/us Those in need of help from abuse: https://takebackthenight.org/ 1(800)656-HOPE, National Sexual Violence Resource Center, NSVRC.org https://www.nsvrc.org/ RAINN Rape, Abuse & Incest National Network Call 1-800-656-4673

- Do you believe anything you listed could be holding you back?

_____

_____

_____

_____

_____

- How have you dealt with these trials? Was it in a healthy manner?

_____

_____

_____

_____

_____

- Have you handled things differently than others who you know faced similar issues?

_____

_____

_____

_____

_____

- Can you draw any connections between your behavior and your past? I.e. the appearance of your inner child?

_____

_____

_____

_____

_____

Steps Towards Change

To begin, I want to express that I am in no way making light of the idea that changing one's life, especially after years of living as we have, is a difficult task. Particularly if you have to rein in an addiction. As someone who was an alcoholic for a majority of her life before achieving sobriety, I now know that what I previously thought unattainable, is honestly possible. Already a formidable task, it's not surprising that once we reach a certain age or point in life we mistakenly believe it to be an impossible goal.

The idea that our age is a factor when it comes to change is a complete fabrication that has been woven into our belief system over time; for there is proof that so many people have changed their lives later in life. It is also a fallacy that there is a one-way street, so to speak, in how a person should go about changing their lives. For many of us this misconception more than likely leads us to giving up in discouragement. In addition to these misconceptions, is the challenge of our environment that we encounter when making the decision to change, particularly those whom we have dedicated our lives to being comfortable in the status quo. Therefore, I take time to explore a few of these relevant issues when it comes to changing our lives for the better and the hurdles that confront us.

The nature of how we go about changing our direction in

life is of vital importance. Something that can be rather oblique, for it can require finding a way to circumvent many pitfalls when it comes to a set routine and even more so discovering what works for you. Beginning with the formerly mentioned, once we find ourselves in a moment of clarity with the desire to make a change in our lives, it may not always be just about you. This can be problematic when it comes to changing one's life, maybe even more so than change itself. Because we might find ourselves in a place that others rely on us to uphold. We might have a partner and/or loved ones that have become complacent or just comfortable in a norm that you want to break. Perhaps your spouse and loved ones are dependent upon your daily routines that coincide with theirs or are rather controlling in various aspects of your life, in which case revealing this desire could be problematic. Whatever your particular challenge is, it will most likely involve the need to alter your mindset, which cannot be properly accomplished without critical thinking.

However, if you are truly dedicated to wanting change in your life, you must emphasize this to your loved ones, knowing that it is okay to take time out for you and to concentrate on yourself and your needs. This is not an inherently selfish choice as many would have you believe, so long as you approach it with respect to others. When we better ourselves, we also empower our loved ones to do the same by spending time with them and providing the authentic attention they deserve from us. Rather than being present physically but not mentally, because we are preoccupied with our lack of fulfillment. And as I have previously mentioned, TIME is our most valuable gift of all; the only thing we truly own and therefore the only thing we can give that matters. Considering this outlook, only reinforces the importance of taking the time to provide yourself a healthy life that can be better appreciated and shared with our loved ones.

When deciding to introduce change and growth into your life, it's also just as important to acknowledge what you can't change. We make no progress when we become preoccupied with the things we can't change or focusing on how we believe things *should* be. All this perspective offers is a distraction and it's something to keep in mind when seeking a new path in your life.

- What expectations do you have of yourself and your future?

_____

_____

_____

_____

_____

- Is your outlook realistic?

_____

_____

_____

_____

_____

- Now, take some time to recognize and contemplate what might be hindering your prospects.

_____

_____

_____

_____

_____

- Where is your attention directed? Towards things you can or cannot change?

_____

_____

_____

_____

_____

Finding The Right Method For You

"It is common sense to take a method and try it. If it fails, admit it frankly and try another. But above all, try something." – Franklin D. Roosevelt

One thing I noticed most in books and speeches that seek to inspire change, is a set routine which one should follow and adhere to in order to reach their goals. Heeding another's instructions isn't always a pathway to success and can easily end in failure. For it is not necessary that we conform to another's version of the *right* way; it is our own path we are here to seek.

I stress this point because I know how hard it is to find help and even if you do, the assistance you find might not work. It is therefore, worthy of your time and effort, especially for those of you who feel self-defeated, to find a system that works for you. Finding the right method that benefits you is key; it may take several attempts to discover the right fit or alternatively, create your own, regardless, do not give up. I have always taken my own path, preferring it to others' and in the end, things have consistently had a way of working out for me. You must find what routine gels with you, taking into consideration what restrictions you face - mental, physical, financial, the support you have, your schedule and so forth. Being that we all live such diverse lives, it's no wonder that a cookie cutter method cannot be applied to everyone's life.

Just remember that not everything changes over night, slow and steady wins the race. And while I am not in any way encouraging the continued use of bad habits, what I am saying is that change takes time. In fact, attempting to do too much all at once can prevent us from flourishing by introducing a too dominating and overbearing routine we aren't prepared for. While some people are capable of doing so, not all of us are and that's okay. So, take one step at a time and it will lead you in the right direction. Start with something small; I chose to seek a new outlet by getting a punching bag. Typical exercise never helped me relieve my adrenalin and frustration as it does for others, but this option worked perfectly! To begin, make a plan of your daily goals. It's a simple task but it can prove inspirational to meet them, especially for those who struggle with routine or pursuing their aspirations. Even crossing the mundane off your list incites a feeling of accomplishment and with it, a confidence to strive towards higher aspirations.

- Analyze your coping methods, is there anything that you should get rid of that is not working, or perhaps anything you could try to do differently that might heal some old wounds?

_____

_____

_____

_____

_____

- What outlets do you utilize, if any?

_____

_____

_____

_____

_____

- Have you incorporated any unorthodox methods for bringing about change? If not, can you think of any possibilities that might aid you?

_____

_____

_____

_____

_____

Boundaries

The idea of 'boundaries' is common enough, yet establishing and maintaining them can be a difficult task. Boundaries set the terms for how we live life and experience our relationships. When I speak of boundaries, I am referring to, of course, the limits we establish in our interactions with others but also those that help define us as an individual. I'll begin with the latter concept.

Having boundaries is not only necessary to keep our relationships healthy, but ourselves as well; it's a type of self-care that reinforces our self-worth and self-respect. It's important to keep this in mind for when you encounter those who would label it as a purely selfish behavior and aim to make you feel ashamed so that you will conform to their own expectations and securities.

Growing up, for many of us, our family represents our worldview. Naturally, as the years pass we become more independent and secure in our worth as an individual, or at least that's the general expectation. But for just as many, the notion of family becomes wholly encompassing, a view encouraged by the family themselves, limiting a person's ability to distinguish themselves from the pack. These dynamics I am speaking of place heavy emphasis on putting other members first (not an intrinsically negative concept), even at the expense of one's own happiness or wellbeing. As to be expected over time, being raised without an introduction to boundaries, leads to the inclination to automatically consider the welfare of others before oneself, an aspect that follows into all relationships, friends and romances alike.

Establishing and owning our identity is necessary to living a satisfying life and in itself is the most important boundary of all. An unfortunate consequence of being taught to give your all to others is the negation of developing as your own person. Entering adulthood after such a childhood can leave us feeling lost, unaware of our own desires, and developing relationships that would once again represent our identity. The road to change for these individuals will inevitably require a path of self-exploration and the testing of new boundaries with others, a fact that can be more difficult later in life.

When it comes to not erecting boundaries, many of us are guilty and the prevention can range through an assortment of reasoning. Some of us feel intimidated at the idea, misbelieving that to do so is an insult to those we love. But broaching the topic of what troubles you and asking the person in question to respect it is perfectly acceptable. Of course, it helps if the relationship in question is open and honest, so that the discussion can reflect that. If that is in fact not the case, then the thought of raising the topic is another cause for intimidation in itself.

Determining what boundaries are needed with our relationships begins with identifying your expectations and needs. We all expect certain aspects and behaviors from our loved ones. Obviously when these expectations are met it's smooth sailing but when we find that a certain behavior irritates us, the next step is to decide what we want to do about it. Is the action in question bearable or does it completely cross the line? Only you can answer this question, dependent as it is to the circumstances and the individuals involved.

To answer these questions, it's necessary to evaluate just what exactly you require from others. Give thought to who you are as a person, what you represent, what behavior or morals coincide with your own beliefs, not limited to religion or politics. When you are familiar with where you stand with yourself, you can better identify exactly how you feel on matters so that you can take a firm stance behind them by enacting boundaries. This allows you to stay true to who you are and not compromise your feelings or beliefs over a misunderstanding or lack of communication. But this process also includes recognizing the history of your relationships and what you've allowed to slide by; when you allowed it to occur, you inadvertently told the other person it was okay. Reviewing your past interactions with others may inspire feelings of resentment, being taken advantage of, hurt and anger, or a revelation that the relationship is unhealthy and not what you thought it was.

Remember not to assume anything of others or yourself. We cannot act under the assumption that others should automatically be aware of our thoughts or preferences for any reason, such as presuming others to act as we would, it's the 'obvious and expected' thing to do, or to think others should figure it out on their own. These expectations of behavior frequently lead to disappointment, resentment, and fractures in the relationship. I can personally attest to the damage of not imposing boundaries and expecting different behavior, can have on relationships as well as ourselves. I'd never heard the term boundary in this context until I first visited a therapist at the age of 23 and regrettably I did not take the advice to heart.

Geared with this information, the next step is putting your boundary into clear words and communicating them. How we go about this is pertinent to the success of the outcome. A great many of us have experienced doing this incorrectly, often because we let the behavior continue for too long without ever considering our expectations properly and in an instant of temper snapped out at the offending person. Of course, in the heat of the moment, your wishes aren't articulated politely or clearly, and a squabble likely ensues. Other times you might express your preference in passing without elaborating your reasoning or feelings. Neither of these are an example of marking a boundary. Implementing boundaries requires a clear and precise explanation of your feelings, needs, and expectations delivered in a calm and non-accusatory manner. Doing so requires patience on your part as well as an openness so those in question can fully understand where you are coming from, how you feel, why you need these restrictions, and what behavior you will and will not consent to.

There will naturally be opposition at times when you broach this subject, whether it's with a healthy, new, or established relationship. As I previously mentioned, bringing up behaviors with those who've we tolerated them from for years is not an easy task. Allowing the bad behavior to continue for so long creates both resentment in you and in the one who is suddenly being asked to change their behavior. It does not hurt to acknowledge to your loved one, your complicity in the dynamic that's persisted over time, hopefully easing the strain that could rear up a defensive response.

For example, my father had a habit of randomly showing up to my house without calling first. I've always found this to be an inconvenience because I might be busy, taking a shower, or not dressed but particularly when I was taking online college courses, requiring timed tests meaning I couldn't be disturbed. It was also something I never did to others, to just show up without their permission or giving any notice. When I tried communicating the situation to him, his response was always, "don't you love me." It quickly became apparent that this was not a behavior he would change, perhaps because from back in his day it was an accepted and common behavior. Realizing this, I then had to make the decision if I could simply put up with it and I found that I could. I knew this habit of his wasn't coming from a disrespectful place, he just didn't understand so it enabled me to not take it personally and handle it in the best manner possible.

When you do make the decision to introduce your boundary, you have to do so with a commitment to see that it's honored. Yet there will be instances, like I had with my father, that you decide that it's tolerable. Outside of these cases, the best you can do is inform your loved one of your expectations and calmly insist that the continuation of the behavior will not be allowed. Predictably, after agreeing to your stance, mistakes may be made while they are learning to acquiesce to your new expectations, understandably so, as it's an adjustment period. However, when these instances arise, immediately inform them that they crossed the line that you've drawn and if need be, remove yourself from their presence until they can respect you and what you've requested.

Those who love and respect you will immediately or eventually yield with the boundaries you've set but not everyone will be receptive to your feelings and needs. You might have to cut ties with those who refuse to acknowledge the importance of and comply with your limits, or at the very least, set your own boundaries in place so that you can deal with the situations that arise. This may mean, that you leave an event early if it's with the person in question. Or plan ahead, making note that if A or B transpires, decide to leave in case such an event occurs or know how you will handle the situation appropriately. Another example might be where to decide to meet up with those who could cross your boundaries, especially ones that could impede on your recovery. Take for instance when I quit drinking, I had to distance myself from my brother and his girlfriend; she was a heavy drinker, starting early and not stopping till night. Therefore, when I met up with them, it was only for breakfast at a location that did not serve alcohol. This boundary allowed me to continue to make positive choices that enabled my sobriety. On the flip side, my brother attempted to quit drinking on many occasions, but staying in a relationship with someone who drank everyday meant he never instituted a boundary that helped him reach his goals.

As you see, when this involves family, it can seem a near impossible decision to make. I would ponder to guess that the family unit can and is the most destructive when it comes to people instigating change in their lives. I know from personal experience that our families can be dominating and not readily open to new or expansive ideologies. But don't forget that you shouldn't have to sacrifice your respect, well-being, security, or happiness for another to maintain a relationship. If it's necessary, then the circumstances are simply not healthy.

Making the decision to change your life is a process that will undoubtedly require implementing boundaries and in doing so you need to have an open dialogue with your loved ones; explain to them in calm terms that you need your time and your desire to change certain aspects of your life. Do your best to get them to be supportive of you and even join you, but also be readily aware that this support might not be garnered and that it may be necessary to find an alternative outlet on your path towards change. Therefore, to really change your life, you may need to make some very uncomfortable changes first, so that you can concentrate solely on you and your journey.

- Do you know who are? Are you comfortable with yourself as individual?

_____

_____

_____

_____

_____

- Are your relationships healthy?

_____

_____

_____

_____

_____

- Do you know what your boundaries are? What are they? If you don't, give it some serious thought and write them down.

_____

_____

_____

_____

_____

- Do you sometimes feel others in your relationships cross a metaphorical line?

_____

_____

_____

_____

_____

- How have you responded when this happens? Does it make you feel taken advantage of or inspire anger?

_____

_____

_____

_____

_____

- Do you feel you could benefit from instilling boundaries?

_____

_____

_____

_____

_____

Triggers

Whether you are trying to change a behavior in particular or just your mindset in general, it's imperative to identify what is provoking the negative action or attitude in the first place. In other words, your triggers. Everyone has pet peeves or idiosyncrasies that get under their skin, but for some it leads less towards simple irritation and instead induces an intensely negative reaction.

Identifying triggers is also an essential part of staying on point. All too often we are functioning on autopilot; so, we are not conscious of our decisions, which means you must work at being in the present moment. This doesn't happen for all of us overnight, it takes work. Repetition is key; the more we do - the more easily we do it, and so on. While making this change, awareness of what our triggers are is critical.

For many, an individual's trigger is related to a past trauma they experienced, one that is still within them and perhaps never dealt with properly. The onset can be sudden and unanticipated, quickly striking one's nerves and evoking a reaction such as a flashback. Make no mistake, these instances can be quite powerful, manipulating our mental, emotional, and physical states. The trigger can be correlated to any of the five senses we experience, giving us an instant replay of an event. Perhaps it's a smell or word, that upon hearing it brings us back to the trauma itself. Flashbacks can be as harrowing as the original event, entrapping us in its intensity; not surprisingly panic attacks are an expected reaction, but the effects of these situations can also manifest themselves in how we interact with those surrounding us at the time.

The association between triggers and trauma is not the case for everyone. For many, the reason we develop triggers lies in, naturally, how we are raised. In fact, happy childhoods are not an exception to this trait; it's the lack of adversity in our youth that makes us unprepared for it in the future. That absence means we are not learning the coping skills that one would develop in the learning process. Entering adulthood without that experience can lead to the creation of unhealthy reactions. This isn't the rule for everyone; humans are adaptable, and they learn even if it's later on in life.

When I look back now, it is hard to understand why such little trivial matters would set me off, but they did. It was intense, my body literally felt the stress of the issue even if it was petty; I could feel the tingling sensation rip throughout my being, urging me to drink to relieve it. It had become routine and so deeply ingrained in me that I would not even consider another alternative. As I previously mentioned, I was never taught or truly understood what triggers were and therefore did not correlate my sudden urge for a quick fix to a cause that I could identify. Growing up life was relatively good and as such, I was never taught how to handle bad things that arose. Therefore, anything upsetting in nature, whether big or small, sent me into a panic and drinking became my outlet.

My triggers instigated my need for alcohol but how triggers influence us differs greatly from person to person. Regardless of those differences, it's a reaction that becomes ingrained in our behavior. This habit persisted because I chose not to live in the moment and take control of my responses; in doing so, I essentially taught myself to replicate the behavior. Now comes the reprogramming, teaching ourselves what should have been instilled in us from an early age and unlearning our bad habits.

- Can you identify anything that systematically causes an irrational or negative behavior on your part?

_____

_____

_____

_____

_____

- What type of reaction does your trigger provoke?

_____

_____

_____

_____

_____

• What are some alternatives you can turn to when presented with your trigger?

_____

_____

_____

_____

_____

Change Begins

Change begins when we choose to change - plain and simple.

For those who struggle in their daily lives, whether it's with routine, a mental disorder, or a familial dysfunction, etc., it's not uncommon to bemoan the fact that they don't live a "normal" life. We seem to create this ideal in our mindset that the majority of society must live by a certain standard, perpetuated by the continuous barrage of perfect lifestyles fed to us through entertainment, social media, and the media. But it's vital to remember that there is no "normal." Everyone has struggles that vary considerably from person to person and how they deal with them is no less diverse. So many self-help gurus urge people to live their best life. This is no doubt a worthy goal and we tell ourselves that we want to achieve it, but we still lose sight of the key word: live **YOUR** best life. This is not a quest for perfection; do not measure happiness by a perceived ideal. Such a thing is unobtainable, but happiness isn't. Yet, when we cry for the loss of this normalcy we are automatically putting ourselves down. We cannot truly become our best selves when our vision of it inherently negates our self-worth and therefore the progress we make. We are human, we will mess up, and this trait that we all share is as close to normal as you can get. While fighting in our pursuit of change and growth, this is the most important thing to keep in mind. Discouragement and self-doubt can be the biggest hurdle in the search for happiness.

Our top priority when it comes to change, is to set forth in our goals. To awake each morning and get busy fulfilling those goals so we can check them off our list as accomplished! What we do not want to do, is overthink; doing so opens the door to self-doubt thus moving us in the wrong direction. All too often our overthinking can make us stagnant. Why? Because it overwhelms us. Dwelling in our thoughts holds us back, redirects our motives, and good intentions, and undermines our course. Over evaluating impedes your motivation; sometimes it's better to just stop thinking and do.

Prioritizing and redirecting one's focus is essential to making progress. But to do so, it may mean reprogramming your coping skills and that starts with adjusting one's way of thinking. I've often noticed that when I begin my day by immediately working, instead of contemplating my schedule first, I have better success in achieving what I've set out to do. This is a big advantage for those of us who suffer with depression, stress, anxiety, or fear, because instead of allowing our minds to rule us, we shut them down and get busy. I cannot express how deeply this has changed my life; focusing on my determination as opposed to allowing negativity to captivate my mind makes a world of difference. For instance, in the past I might've told myself, "oh not today, maybe tomorrow." And then tomorrow comes and goes just as easily as it arrived and there I am, once again, digitally programing my mind; keeping my stress at bay by procrastinating.

As I am writing this, I can honestly say that my bouts with depression that have dominated much of life, have been evaporating for quite some time now. I believe this is a result of my thinking habits as well as my determination to stop questioning everything and just accomplishing my missions. Our effort now is to change our mindset, and this will indeed take continuous effort on our parts.

- What obstacles do you face in making the changes you desire?

_____

_____

_____

_____

_____

- What are some easy transitions you can begin to make to lead towards those changes?

_____

_____

_____

_____

_____

Thinking Habits

This brings us to the idea that once we change our thoughts, we can change our lives; this is not a fabrication ~ indeed, it's a very real truth. Negative thoughts are an extremely inhibiting factor in life. Why is it that we all think so negatively? It is not only counterproductive, but crippling more times than not, our minds control us, rather than us controlling our minds. For instance, many of us tend to second-guess ourselves and to consider our past failures rather than our past successes.

So, what is it we need to do? The answer lies in regaining control of our thoughts and mind process. Our minds are incredibly powerful; yet, we often function on autopilot. We do not necessarily need to be present in the moment to accomplish our daily routine. In this and other ways, we are operating not so differently from the robots we create. The key difference is, we have the ability to control our minds ~ if we choose to, that is.

Dr. Joe Dispenza speaks about this in his book *Breaking the Habit of Being Yourself*, as well as in the documentary *What the Bleep Do We Know!?*, and in his many speeches.[14] Dr. Dispenza's teachings are based on our thinking habits and in how we move forth towards natural progression through our

---

[14] For more information visit https://drjoedispenza.com/

thinking patterns. What we think we create, and therefore what we focus on and how we control our thoughts and direct our attention is essential - if we are to truly change our destiny and reclaim control over our lives.

To enumerate on the idea of how powerful our thoughts can be, think of it like this: it is common for people to overthink, which then leads us to becoming over worried, and thus we often become overwhelmed. This, in and of itself, is a paralyzing progression that leads us down an unhealthy path in life; not only diverting us from our true destiny but negatively manifesting itself in our health. Our minds are extremely sensitive to our feelings; whatever emotion is set off, is instantly connected and the programing is in full automatic operation. Hence, you need to remove all negative judgements; repeat positive thoughts to yourself over and over again throughout the day until it really sinks in. It is not good enough to just say positive affirmations once a day, you need to truly indoctrinate it into your being by making it a routine.

The best way I learned to reprogram my negative and depressed mindset was in repeatedly saying positive affirmations to myself while completing daily chores; I say them while washing the dishes, mowing the lawn, swimming, or taking a shower. Another thing I have learned to do is that when negative messages come my way, I pay attention and ask myself why it's come to me. Is what I am thinking true? And if it is, I ask to forgive myself, knowing that everyone makes mistakes; to err is human, we cannot learn and grow unless we make them.

Therefore, whenever you hear your mind starting to doubt or reiterate all your past disappointments, halt all thinking and redirect the mind to something productive to occupy your time. Remind yourself to focus on your successes; go over them, write them down on a chalkboard or make poster boards for each room, and listen to inspirational music and speeches. In no way am I advising you to ignore your instincts when I say to quiet your mind, for I strongly believe in them. Just know there is a difference between intuitive messages that come to you that should be given credence and the assault of pessimistic thoughts that hold you back. Eventually, focusing and putting forth your effort, will have a great impact on your mind and you will see the results.

Changing our thinking habits isn't limited to redirecting one's thoughts, it also calls for altering the stance one takes in the mental process. Taking the time to delve into one's past does little good if the approach never changes its perspective. Try to introduce objectivity into your mindset to gain clarity. Sometimes we are too close to the subject to see clearly; it can prevent us from admitting our mistakes, acknowledging the damage we've borne, and viewing behavior and relationships for what they truly are, effectively keeping us stuck in an oblivious state. Reaching that objective standpoint is not always so simple; reach out to others for advice and opinions, whether it's through friends or professional sources.

Whatever it is you seek in life – it is yours for the taking; you just need to know this as a fact! No questions asked, no critiquing, no doubt, just full-blown belief and eventually you will really believe it because the proof will come to fruition.

On that note, over time, the more we can focus on being in the moment, the more awareness we will achieve and so it will become our natural way of being.

- Do you tend to overthink and if yes, what types of thoughts consume you? I.e. Are they self-deprecating? Are they centered on complaints, big or small?

_____

_____

_____

_____

_____

- Ask yourself, are these ruminating thoughts useful?

_____

_____

_____

_____

_____

- Do you struggle to think objectively? If so, can you turn to someone to give yourself an alternative point of view?

_____

_____

_____

_____

_____

Once you identify them, they're easier to recognize when they cross your mind, so you can nip them in the bud!

Goals

Let us take a moment for you to write down your goals. Often people ask us to set goals for the current year and what our goals are for the next five or ten years. There is no problem in during so, but the most important plan setting is that of daily goals. Why? Because this is where we will see real progress or not. It is kind of funny to think of now, but I recall my mother making fun of my eldest sister and I for always making a To Do List. Mom always just did what needed to be done. But as for myself, my bouts of depression and constant addiction meant that accomplishing daily chores presented itself as more of a struggle. And while I might have been able to accomplish yearly goals I had set in place, this did not always extend to my day-to-day expectations. I struggled with everyday chores; getting to work always felt like an uphill climb, after that, the typical agenda of daily errands, housework, and what not, was not even on my radar. But what I have since learned is that by setting my day-to-day goals means I pay specific attention to them; even when I do not always fulfill them, it leads me to accomplishing more than I would, had I not kept track.

First off, don't go overboard; now there is nothing wrong with planning for the years ahead, but separate them into daily, monthly, yearly and so on, so as not to overextend yourself. As you move forward and mark off your accomplishments, make special note of them, and place them as reminders for yourself. This is essential as many of us are more likely to look at past failures rather than past achievements, and this leads towards discouragement and distraction getting in our way. Therefore, you need to reassure yourself of those accomplishments; this will become a significant motivational factor in your life, propelling you to keep moving towards your pursuits and further inspiring you as you meet your accomplishments. And in order for us to keep up with our goals we need to be motivated!

- What are your goals?

_____

_____

_____

_____

_____

- Are you still in pursuit of your goals?

_____

_____

_____

_____

_____

- What steps have you taken to achieve them?

_____

_____

_____

_____

_____

Motivation

Creating plans and methods to achieve our goals is all well and good, but no manner of planning can compensate for a lack of motivation. For myself and many others, it is one of the biggest hindrances in advancing one's life, often due to our procrastination. As I've been saying all along, search for what will best inspire you; what works for one person may have no effect on another.

The main motivator for me is undoubtedly music. *I Will Survive* by Gloria Gaynor, *The Man in the Mirror* by Michael Jackson, or *Let Your Love Flow* by the Bellamy Brothers are just some of my go-to songs. When I find that I'm feeling sluggish, music acts as a fantastic stimulus that energizes me. Not only does it revitalize my body, but it brings about a positive mind frame, both improving my mood and giving me the confidence to tackle whatever I need to accomplish.

As a mother, I've always found my daughter to be a source of inspiration, as most parents generally do. Naturally, I have photos of her and of my loved ones scattered around and on my desk as a reminder, but I make sure to look at them every morning, afternoon, and night, to ensure they stay at the forefront of my thoughts, keeping me motivated. Too often we lose touch with our surroundings and just go through the motions; therefore, take the time to bring focus to your life and relish in the moment.

Reading is a key ingredient in both boosting my energy and inspiring my mindset. But more than just finding inspiration, it's also just as important to identify what keeps us complacent. Why is reading so important? Well, in my opinion reading is important primarily because it allows us to expand our awareness, opening our minds to messages from an outside source. While obtaining my masters, I would wake up in the middle of the night with thoughts rushing through my mind. My intensive reading allowed ideas to flow to me more readily, usually pertaining towards the 20-page papers I had to write.

Reading doesn't just broaden our awareness, it's also a foundation of quiet in a chaotic world. This peaceful exercise of the brain permits us the opportunity to induce more control over the mind. Reading brings about an internal conversation, regarding both the material in question and ourselves. How we react to what we are reading offers an insight to how our thought process works which is another avenue of growth in itself.

If you don't find these options to your taste, search for what does inspire you. Maybe it's affirmations, creating a vision board, journaling, rewards, or focusing on who or what you are working for. If you have an issue finding a medium that helps center and motivate you, reach out to someone who can offer you some support in maintaining your commitment. Take a moment to meditate on what inspires you and then make a list of what incentives you can incorporate into your life to help you fulfill your goals.

As I mentioned, it's just as, if not more important to adjust what hinders our motivation than finding what inspires us. I cannot stress enough that how we end our day is just as significant as how we begin it. Countless times we go to sleep preoccupied with the negative events of the day. This routine is not only toxic to our drive but to our health as well. Awakening the morning after a night's sleep overrun by cynical thoughts and images, subtly influences how we perceive and act throughout our day. Regardless if we remember or ignore our dream state, the subconscious messages bleed into our waking minds and our interactions along with it.

For me, listening to motivational videos first thing in the morning and as I prepare for bed in the evening has proven to be very influential. A vastly different ritual to the one that used to have me glued to the television. That's right, turn off the TV! Today it has become another form of addiction that serves as a source of escape that diverts us from our goals. I implore you to rein in those bad habits and introduce more moderation into your life. It's a concept that I too have struggled with but have found that my incentives have helped bring it about.

Our sleeping habits leave a powerful impression on the daylight hours. Therefore, it's imperative to introduce a positive and healthy regimen before bed. Try meditating, praying, reviewing what we are grateful for, listening to inspirational speeches, to positive I AMs, or even just relaxing background music. For it will encourage you to awaken the next day with a vivacious zest for life. So, when the evening comes, I find the best method for me is to do stretches, while envisioning my next day and the success of it. By doing so, you program your mind towards the positive, knowing that one day, the negative thoughts will become a thing of the past.

- Do you lack motivation? If yes, what could you do to bring about more inspiration? If no, how can you better direct your motivation to accomplish your goals?

_____

_____

_____

_____

_____

Ending

Once we begin to live and view our lives from a different lens, in other words, seeing the glass as Always Half-Full, this type of mindset will set out to inspire us, keep moving us forward and upwards towards our true destination. Allowing other things not to become a distraction but instead a momentum to push onward. After hearing about my brother's passing, I could have easily slipped into a dark state; instead it actually made me realize that there truly is no time like the Present and while I will continue to cherish my loved ones whom have passed, there was a message that it was time to get Busy! Meant as a Momentum rather than a detour!

And therein lies the simplistic truth of the matter, which is that if we truly want to change we have to keep the pendulum from swinging back and forth, find the middle ground, the peace and solace of life, and learn to heal and forgive, so that we can move towards where we were always meant to be in this world of ours. So that we can inspire ourselves and our loved ones! For us to genuinely live up to our life's potential, dreams, and goals. And by doing so, it helps spread the knowledge and change that is so desperately needed throughout society. *We Are The World* (by Quincy Jones) and we need you; we need all the wonderful people of this world to heal themselves, take charge of their lives and pursue their goals to make this world a better place, for ourselves, for our loved ones, and for future generations to come.

Our unhealthy environment's lack of hope, love, support, and connections, and our pervasive stress and fear provides the perfect breeding ground for it to spread and contaminate. I believe that the more we consume, sedate, deny, and isolate ourselves, the more divided we will and have become. I have come to find my sister's and mother's illness symbolic. Looking at the world as a giant living organism, I see that we are not unlike the parasites that feed on us, that cancer is not just something that resides in our bodies but on our planet as well. No different than the cells in our body, we are the cells that are either vibrant and healthy or sick and destructive. Our personal beings have a greater impact than we realize, expanding and developing from our homes to our communities, workplaces, cultures, beliefs, values, and politics, both individually and collectively ~ in short, the Human Race. Considering this outlook, it's easily concluded that we have a responsibility to become our best selves.

One of the last comments my mother ever made to me was that she knew I would go on to do something great with my life. I cherished this statement from her; I want to make her proud. And although I am not looking for any real recognition or fortune, as I do not believe in either, if my story, my message, and any help I can pass along to others is the Lucky thing I have to offer this world, that is not only good enough for me, but is what I believe I was always meant to do. To not only fulfill my destiny, but perhaps that of my mother and my sister as well, as they too sought for change. My hope for change extends beyond that of personal growth and aspires for unification under honesty, equality, balance, and respect. I wish for everyone to recognize that not only are we all capable of change, we are also all worthy of it as well. We are all One and we are all Worthy of Love, Forgiveness, and Change; so, Make the Change and Live a Better Life!

- What is the primary objective you want to meet?

_____

_____

_____

_____

_____

- Do you feel like you've gained any clarity after taking a magnifying glass to your inner self?

_____

_____

_____

_____

_____

- What decisions have your revelations inspired and how will they prompt you to accomplish your goals?

_____

_____

_____

_____

_____

• Are you ready to Make the Change?

_____

_____

_____

_____

_____

Stay tuned for my upcoming books, *Making the Change: Micro to Macro* and *Making the Change: Social Justice*, and check out my previous autobiography if you are so inclined to learn more about me, *Lucky Penny* available on Amazon.

Printed in the United States
By Bookmasters